For more than forty years,
Yearling has been the leading name
in classic and award-winning literature
for young readers.

Yearling books feature children's
favorite authors and characters,
providing dynamic stories of adventure,
humor, history, mystery, and fantasy.

Trust Yearling paperbacks to entertain,
inspire, and promote the love of reading
in all children.

counting on grace

ELIZABETH WINTHROP

A YEARLING BOOK

Published by Yearling, an imprint of Random House Children's Books
a division of Random House, Inc., New York

Visit us on the Web! www.randomhouse.com/kids

Educators and librarians, for a variety of teaching tools, visit us at
www.randomhouse.com/teachers

ISBN: 978-0-553-48783-1

Reprinted by arrangement with Wendy Lamb Books

Printed in the United States of America

August 2007

20 19 18 17 16 15

First Yearling Edition

For Candy

someone to be counted on . . .

If I could tell the story in words,
I wouldn't need to lug around a camera.

— *Lewis Hine*

SCHOOL

"Grace, your turn."

The book is called *The Red Badge of Courage*. I like that name. I stand up to read, but as soon as I open my mouth, my feet start moving. It always happens that way. I can't help it.

" 'The youth was in a little trance of astonishment. So they were at last going to fight.' Miss Lesley, why don't the youth have a name?"

"Why *doesn't* the youth have a name," Miss Lesley says, but I go right on. She's always trying to fix our grammar, but we don't pay much mind.

"The writer should call him Joe or Henry or something."

In the front row, my little brother, Henry, giggles. Miss Lesley touches his head with her hand and he stops. At least she don't smack him with that ruler of hers.

"Grace, sit down when you read."

"I can't. I don't read as good. When I sit my brain stops working."

"Nonsense. Your brain works just like everybody else's. I want you to stay in one place when you read. Stop hopping around the room. Look at Arthur. He can sit still. Now you try it."

Arthur's desk is hooked up to mine and he never moves a muscle 'cepting his lips when he's reading. That's why Miss Lesley likes him the best. It's not only 'cause he's the best reader. It's 'cause he's a sitter and the rest of us are hoppers, jumpers, fidgeters. Arthur's twelve too, but he's four months older than me. I can read just as good as him so long as I can move around at the same time.

I go on. " 'He could not accept with asshur—' "

"Assurance," Miss Lesley says. "That means he could not believe. Henry, sit up and listen. Your sister's reading a story."

I finish the sentence. " '. . . he was about to mingle in one of those great affairs of the earth.' "

"Thank you, Grace. Please sit now. What do you think that means? Class?"

Arthur's hand goes up. Miss Lesley nods at him.

"The youth's going to be in a war."

"How do you know that?"

"I read ahead."

Arthur always reads ahead.

"And if you hadn't read ahead, Arthur?"

" 'Cause there are soldiers in the story. If there are soldiers, there's gonna be a war."

"Right. This is a story about the Civil War. Some of you

2

children could have had grandparents who fought in that war."

"Not me," says Dougie. "My grandparents lived in Ireland."

"Me either," yells Felix. "My grandparents were born in Canada."

Miss Lesley claps her hands for silence. The whole time she's teaching, Miss Lesley moves around the room, keeping us kids in order. I'm back at my desk, but my feet are dancing underneath. Miss Lesley slaps them with her ruler whenever she passes by. I pretend I don't even feel it. Seems she cares more about sitting still than learning.

"You older children go on reading among yourselves now. One sentence each, then pass the book."

I hate that. I like to hear my voice doing the reading. Or Arthur's. Thomas mumbles so you can't understand him and Norma just pretends to read and Rose is too busy twirling her hair around her finger and staring at Thomas. I hate when the story goes too slow. Then I forget what's happening.

It's Arthur who's reading when we hear footsteps outside on the wooden porch, the thunk of a boot against the step to knock off the mud. We get still. The man coming through that door understands that Miss Lesley don't like dirt in her classroom.

We know who it is. We know what he's going to say. I sneak a peek at Arthur, who's put the book down. For once.

Miss Lesley has her ruler raised and suddenly she stops moving too.

The door opens. French Johnny pokes his head in first, almost like a little kid asking permission. He went to this school himself. He knows how hard the benches can be after a day of sitting. He knows every hook by the door and the way the handle of the coal stove wriggles out and slams to the floor when someone ain't paying mind. French Johnny is the second hand at the mill. He's in charge of the spinning room where my mother runs six frames. He's come up the hill in his white apron to get a mill rat. That's what they call the kids who work in the mill. We all end up as mill rats.

"Yes?" Miss Lesley says with no respect in her voice. She might as well be talking to a second grader like my brother, Henry.

"Come for the boy," says French Johnny. He sounds like he don't want to be here. He knows she won't let this one go without a fight. Truth is she argues with him over every single one of us.

"Well, you can turn around and walk right out of here. You're not taking him," says Miss Lesley, keeping her back to barrel-bellied French Johnny. She's acting as if he's no bigger than one of those sow bugs come out of the woodwork this time of year. "Class, I want you to pay attention to the board. We're going to make the sound of these two letters." Her ruler smacks the *CH*. "Chuh," she says to the younger ones. "Repeat after me. Chuh."

But nobody says nothing. We're all waiting and watching French Johnny.

4

"Chuh," she says again, her voice rising. She's getting angry.

Nobody speaks.

I can't stand silence like that.

"Chuh," I say, and two of the little kids laugh.

French Johnny is all the way in the room now. He's squirmed around the door and closed it behind him.

He signals to Arthur, who pays him no mind.

"Monsieur Jean," says Miss Lesley. "You have not been invited into my classroom."

"Now, Miss Lesley, don't give me trouble this morning. You know he's got to go. He's the only man left in the house now, and his mother needs him to doff her frames. He'll come back when the work slacks off."

Miss Lesley whirls around. Her eyes are shooting fire. "You say that every time. I do believe lying is still considered a sin in your religion and in mine, *monsieur*." The way she says *mister* in French makes it sound dirty and French Johnny flinches almost like *he's* been smacked with the ruler. "The work never slacks off."

"In the summer when the river drops, it does," says French Johnny. But we all know that's lame. That's not going to get him anywhere with Miss Lesley.

"Do you have papers for him?" she asks. "You know the law, don't you, *monsieur*? No children under the age of fifteen while school is in session? Where are his papers?" She's facing him full on now. "Don't take me for a fool, *monsieur*." That dirty word again. The ruler rises up, points at his belly. *"The work is never going to slack off."* She takes a step toward him.

5

French Johnny holds his ground, but he's keeping an eye on her.

"Arthur Trottier is my best student. He could be a teacher or a manager or even a lawyer someday. So long as you leave him be. Because we both know the only way he will ever come back to this school is when your machine spits him out. Like Thomas there."

Without turning or even looking behind her, she moves the ruler around until it's pointing at Thomas Donahue, the biggest boy in the class, who's scrunching himself down in the back row trying to hide.

All heads swing with the ruler as if we got no power on our own to decide where our eyes should go.

Last summer Thomas was fooling around when they were moving a big new spinning frame into the room. He slipped in the grease and the gearbox got rolled right over his bare foot. By the time they lifted it off him, harm was already done.

Thomas spent three months at home. His foot healed all crooked and he walks on the side of it now. Makes him lean far over just to walk and he falls a lot. No use for him at the mill no more.

He hates school. I hear him talking about running away, but that would be mighty hard with a foot that curls around under itself like a fern coming out in the spring.

Now French Johnny decides he's going to pretend Miss Lesley ain't there. They've been through all this before. Every time the overseer sends him up the hill to collect another child, Miss Lesley acts as if one of her arms is getting chopped off.

"Let's go, boy," he says.

"Arthur, you stay right there," she says, not taking her eye off French Johnny.

Arthur's gone back to reading our book. He's thinking, Maybe if I pretend this ain't happening, then it ain't.

I know he wants to stay in school. He's not like me or the other boys. Dougie is counting the days, begging his father to send him down the hill even though he's only nine.

I want to go too 'cause of the money I can make. Ever since my father got sick four years ago, we've been behind in the store bills.

But Arthur is different. If reading like a machine makes you smart, then he's the smartest person I ever knew. Arthur hates noise, too many people around, loud games. I could give you a whole list of ways Arthur is different from the other boys. The only thing in the world that Arthur loves besides his mother is books.

His father died of the pneumonia last winter. That's why French Johnny come for him. Arthur and his mother live in mill housing up on French Hill like most of the rest of us. You can't stay in a mill house unless every able-bodied person works. Arthur's twelve, long past time for him to go in.

"Boy, no trouble now," says French Johnny, his voice raised a notch. "Come along quiet."

Arthur lifts his head from the page and looks at Miss Lesley.

"Do I have to go?" he asks.

The silence is so big it could make us all deaf. For just a moment. Then from the back row, one of the big girls calls out in an Arthur voice.

7

"Do I have to go?"

Dougie picks it up. "Miss Lesley, do I have to go?"

"Quiet," says Miss Lesley. The ruler hits the nearest desk, two inches from my brother Henry's nose. He's calling out with the rest of them.

But there's nothing Miss Lesley can do. The chanting gets bigger, like some kind of balloon blowing up in the room, pushing out all the other air.

"Children," Miss Lesley screams. Normally she don't need to raise her voice. So now we know she's lost the fight. This is the one fight she's always going to lose.

Arthur gets up suddenly. The taunting fades almost as fast as it started. We all watch as he snakes his way between the desks and flies out across the front porch, like some kind of trapped animal who just found his cage door standing open.

For a big man, French Johnny can move pretty quick. Suddenly he's gone too.

I look over at Arthur's desk. He left most everything behind. Except the book. The book we were all reading.

～

Miss Lesley's got her back to us and she ain't speaking. Her shoulders are moving up and down. I think maybe she's crying, but there's no noise coming from her. This is worse than her screaming. Nobody knows what to do.

My body is vibrating, I've been sitting so long. I get up and start to dance a little. Now everybody's looking my way.

I figure this is a good thing 'cause I'm giving Miss Lesley time to collect herself.

"It's not so bad, Miss Lesley," I say, sliding past two desks. "He took the book with him. Arthur is never going to give up his reading, no matter where he goes."

"Sit down, Grace," she says, and her voice is low and quiet again.

"We all got to go in sometime. My sister Delia gets her own spinning frames soon. Any day now I'm going to start doffing for my mother." My voice just rattles on sometimes. Follows my feet. Times like these, I can't seem to control either one.

"Why don't you start now?" says Miss Lesley. Her voice has some kind of menace in it.

I can't be hearing her right.

"They don't need me yet," I say. "But don't you see it's a good thing? I'm going to be making extra money so we can buy me my own pair of shoes and I won't have to share with Delia no more. And Henry can get a pair of his own so he won't have to wear those broken-down ones Felix's mother give us to use for Mass."

All eyes turn to my brother in the front row and his bare feet swinging back and forth. He makes them go quiet and glares at me. Any day he can, he runs down the hill barefoot rather than squish himself into my old school shoes.

"You know if I start doffing, then Delia will work her own frame and my mother will still have a doffer and I'll get the two and a half dollars a week and—"

"Get out, Grace." She is not screaming like before, but

she is talking loud. And she's walking toward me as if she's considering running me over. "Go on," she orders. "I'm not going to stand here anymore and wait for that man to snatch another one of my best readers right from under my nose. You want to go doff your mother's machine, then go. *Get out!*"

"But Miss Lesley, I don't mean now—"

"I'll go, Miss Lesley," Dougie yells from his row, but she pays him no mind.

She's done with talking now. She grabs the back of my pinafore with her right hand and pulls it up all into a bunch so's I'm practically choking. Then she steers me out the door of the schoolroom with my feet barely skimming the ground. For a scrawny woman, Miss Lesley is strong when she wants to be.

My mouth is still working around what to say next when I find myself on the wrong side of the door.

All I can think of in that minute is what she called me. Another one of her best readers. Me. Of all people.

2

THE TRAPPER'S SHACK

I stand on that porch thinking. I've never been out in the town before with nowhere special to go. If I'm not in school or at home tending to my grandfather, then I'm at Sunday Mass in the room above the store we use for a church or I'm stopping in at the mill to bring something to my mother or father. But from now on the mill is where I'll be spending every day. What should I do with this little pinch of freedom?

I shouldn't have wondered so long in such a public place.

"Why aren't you in school?" asks a voice.

Madame Boucher has waddled all the way down the hill without my noticing. She calls herself our landlady, but she don't own the house we live in. The mill owners own everything in town—the store, the school and our houses. They hired Madame Boucher to collect the rents on French Hill. Comes for her ninety cents every single Thursday night. Regular as a clock, my father says.

She has airs and calls herself portly. That's just a fake word for fat, especially when your belly swells from the money you make off your own people.

But the worst thing about Madame Portly is she's nosy.

"Answer me," she demands.

"I've been sent to look for Arthur Trottier," I say.

"And why is Arthur not in school?" she asks, but my feet are already dancing off the porch and around the corner of the building, so I can pretend I don't hear her no more.

She is still calling my name when I make my way down the path, but her voice gets fainter and fainter.

⌣

The one place in town you can go without portly women poking into your business is the river.

We live in a little town in the state of Vermont right by the side of the Hoosic—too bad it's not some musical French name like Rivière-du-Loup, which means Wolf River in case you don't know. That's where my grandparents lived in Canada before they come to America.

Pépé, my grandfather, says French is the language of music-making people. Not English. But English is what they speak in America, I tell him.

"Pas pour toi," he grumbles with that thick old pipe stuck in his mouth and the dribble coming down his white beard. We speak French at home, but English *is* for me long as we live in America. In school they laugh at Norma and Felix and the other Franco kids from Canada who still speak with an accent.

12

Miss Sophie, the teacher who used to board with us, said Vermont means green mountain. *Vert* for green, *mont* for *montagne*, which is French for mountain. Miss Sophie learned me to speak English without no accent. In one year, I could speak pretty well. She said I was smart. Then she had to go away 'cause she found a man to marry. That's when we got Miss Lesley as teacher. Four years ago. She boards with a Yankee farmer family a ways out of town. Sometimes the man give her a ride in on his wagon, but mostly she walks to school. Miss Lesley is a Yankee herself. Mamère says she prefers her own people to us Francos. I think Miss Lesley don't care who you are or where you come from long as you sit still.

When Pépé starts in about going home to Canada, my mother says, "Only place to get ahead is here." Truth is her English ain't half bad either, thanks to Miss Sophie. But she's careful not to speak it in front of Pépé.

⌣

The mill needs the river, but the river don't need the mill. The water was flowing along for thousands of years. Then the people come and dammed up the river so it got fatter and the current got strong enough to turn the water-wheel. This time of year in the spring, the river runs high and proud and the wheel never stops, which means the machines got all the power they need. Until the summertime, when the water can go slack.

The river don't seem to mind. Borrow my water, it says. Long as you give it back. Trouble is when the mill spits the water back out, it comes all dirty and it smells queer. Arthur caught me drinking it one time and said it would make me sick. Not me. I've got a stomach that can take anything, even that time I swallowed a rock on a dare.

Arthur's got himself a place down here by the river, a tumbledown old trapper's shack where he hides. If French Johnny didn't catch him going out the door, then that's where Arthur'll be.

You need to push hard to get the door through the brambles and briars growing round it. "Go away," he snaps when I stick my head inside.

"I knew you was going to be hiding here," I tell him. "They'll catch you anyways."

"You going to tell them?" He's curled in the corner, his back against the wet wall, slimy from spring rains. His feet are tucked up close under him and his arms are wrapped around that book like it's his baby or something.

"Course not," I say. "Miss Lesley kicked me out of school."

He cocks his head. "Shhh," he says. "You hear that?"

I listen too. "Just the river going over the rocks. Papa says the water's high even for May."

He winces. Maybe at the word *Papa* 'cause he don't have a father no more to tell him things.

"What are you going to do?" I ask.

"Run away."

"Where to?"

"Massachusetts. Across the border."

I feel a little pinch in my throat. Arthur's not exactly a friend of mine, but he's somebody to talk to.

14

"You going now?"

"Not till after dark," he says. "I'll tell my mother good-bye."

"You're going to leave her?"

I can see he don't like thinking about that.

"Why'd Miss Lesley kick you out of school?" he asks me.

"Said she didn't want French Johnny taking another of her best readers so I might as well leave school right then." I'm proud for him to hear that. "You may be the best reader, but I'm second best."

He shrugs like he don't care.

"It's fine with me," I say. "Least I won't have to sit still all day long waiting on Miss Lesley's ruler."

"You're stupid," Arthur says. "Like the rest."

I don't let people call me names. Ever. My feet are moving before I even think. I start pounding on him, but he just curls up tighter into himself. He don't cover his head with his hands and he don't cry out. I'm the one doing the yelling.

"I am not stupid, Arthur Trottier. You hear me? I am smart just like you. Miss Lesley says so and Miss Sophie before her."

Then a voice behind me says, "Leave him be, girl. I need him in one piece."

It's French Johnny.

Arthur lifts his head and spits at me. "You showed him where I was hid," he screams, gathering himself to bolt again.

"I didn't," I say, backing away. "I didn't show him nothing."

15

French Johnny ain't taking chances this time. He grabs Arthur's arm in one of his big hands. Arthur twists one way, then the other.

"Not her fault, boy. I would have found you anyways. Even without the landlady pointing the way."

But Arthur keeps yelling back at me as French Johnny hauls him up the hill. "I hate you, you tattle."

That's the worst thing anybody can be. A tattle. I've never been that. But Arthur don't believe me. I know he's not ever going to speak to me again.

"Arthur, I'm not a tattle," I yell, but nothing comes back at me 'cept my own echo.

"Pépé," I whisper. And I take off for home, where my grandfather will be waiting. When bad things happen, he's the only one I want near me.

—

Pépé can't work no more. He lies on a bed in the kitchen near the stove, chewing on his pipe. We made him give up his cigarettes so he didn't burn himself up, but we figure the pipe keeps him company and most of the time he forgets to light it anyway. That's a good thing, 'cause there's no extra money for tobacco.

Pépé mostly lives in his bed. Every night we kneel in a circle around him so that he can lead the family rosary and bless us before we sleep. Sundays, Père Alain, our priest, brings him Holy Communion. On Wednesdays after school, I get him *La Justice*, the French newspaper, from Mr.

Dupree at the store. I sit on the edge of the bed and read it to him. He likes to hear me using our language 'cause he knows I've been studying English in school all day.

Truth is Pépé don't know how to read, but long after I'm done he worries away at those pages with his fingers as if touching the words will make them stand up and say their names to him.

The other day, Delia found Pépé walking down the hill to town when he hadn't been out of the kitchen for months. He told her he was going home to Canada and when she tried to lead him back to our house, he pushed her away. Even though Pépé spends most of his time in bed, his arms are still strong from years of plowing. It took two of the men coming up the hill from the mill to coax him home again. When they called him Monsieur *L'Habitant*, that calmed him down 'cause that's the Canadian word for farmer.

But that night he shouted out in his sleep and I heard the squeak of my parents' bed and then my father's voice calming him down. A little later on, Papa pulled out his accordion and played *"Les Bûcherons,"* a song about lumberjacks that always reminds Pépé of home. Pépé must have fallen asleep with the music. I did too.

⌢

When I get home, Pépé is propped up in the corner of his bed, snoring. I tiptoe over to slide the newspaper from between his fingers, but his eyes fly open and he holds tight.

"*Mon petit chou-fleur*," says Pépé. He is always making up names for me. Cauliflower, jewel, bird. "You've come back to see your old Pépé."

"I always come back, Pépé," I say, and I kiss him on both of his leathery cheeks. He smells like stale tobacco and food gone bad. We clean him up real good on Sundays, but this is a Friday.

"So, how was that English school of yours today?"

"Miss Lesley said I'm one of her best readers." I don't tell him all the rest. It's still working itself out in my mind. Pépé is the only one in the family who understands my ways. He don't ask me questions, but if I want to talk, he lets me go on without hushing me.

Truth is in this family, nobody pays either one of us much attention. Going home to Canada is all Pépé ever talks about. And we know he's never going there again. But I let him pretend. And he lets me chatter.

I dip water from the bucket into the kettle for his bowl of tea. In the distance, the whistle blows for the afternoon train. In our town, the noises all come from bells and whistles. There's the mill bell, morning and evening, the opening school bell, the church bells on Sunday and the train whistle four times a day.

The mill stands between the river and the train track and we got to cross those tracks whenever we go to the mill and the store. Every mother in town is always at us about those trains and the Dupree boy who forgot to look and was crushed. Even though that happened years ago before any of us kids was born, the town still talks about it. Strange thing is that boy's little brother, Mr. René Dupree,

18

is the stationmaster now. He also sorts the mail and runs the mill store, where we all buy our supplies.

—

That afternoon whistle always gets Pépé going and he tells me the same story over and over. I don't mind. I want to block out the sound of Arthur screaming that ugly word at me.

Pépé is already talking when I set up the board that holds his tea bowl on his lap. He knocks his pipe against his other hand even though nothing comes out.

"I'll tell you about the time we come down on the train, Grace."

I nod like I never did hear that story before. I watch the whole time he's drinking so the hot tea don't tip over and burn him.

"It was January of 1892, your grandmother, your mother, your father and me."

I lift a spoon of the tea. He sips a little, then waves it away.

"The train carrying us four pulled in next to the mill. It didn't stop but a minute so we barely had time to tumble off onto the platform with all our bundles. Your *grand-mère* wasn't feeling well. I pushed her up the hill in a cart that somebody brought and then I went back down for all our belongings. Nobody took nothing, because there weren't much worth stealing. But that gang of Irish boys in town were waiting on me. They lit out after me and pelted me with their hard ice balls."

19

The Donahue uncles must have been part of that gang. And Dougie and Thomas's father. Dougie is the kind of kid who would have done the same if he'd been born then.

Pépé picks up the bowl of tea and slurps from it. A dribble makes its way down his chin, but I let him be. He don't like me fussing at him when he's telling a story.

"This is no way to start life in a new country is what I told your father when I stumbled in again. I was bone tired from my second trip up that miserable hill and from leaving my farm at such a mighty age and from the blood streaming down out of the cut in the back of my head. 'The Irish don't want us taking away their jobs,' your father told me." Pépé snorts at the idea of that the way he does every time at this point in the story.

But my father was right. The Irish got here before us, but when they started wanting more money, then the mill sent agents up to Québec looking for big Franco-Catholic families to hire.

It was Mamère's idea that she and Papa come down to work in the mills and my father agreed. But they knew they couldn't leave her parents behind.

I never met my *grand-mère* 'cause she died two years after they got here. "Back in Canada, she would have lived," Pépé is always reminding my father. And what can my father say to that?

⌣

Pépé got work that first year in the mill, unloading the bales of cotton. It's the hardest job of all, but he had a

20

strong back and it meant he could be outside. Then when Delia got old enough to go in, he quit for good and took to fishing the river in the summer and keeping the garden. For a while, he peddled vegetables from the back of a wagon to the other mill workers near us and in the larger towns north of ours. He was happy 'cause the growing season was longer in Vermont than back home in Canada. First frost sometimes holds off until October and you can plant by the end of May. After school, me and Henry weeded with him. Henry has the patience of a farmer, Pépé says. Not me. I'm always yanking the carrots out of the dirt before they're ready.

He's nodded off again. I catch the bowl just before his fingers let it go.

The mill bell is ringing. I can hear the workers starting to make their way up French Hill, where we live. There's no Irish Hill or Polish Hill. We're the only ones got a hill named for us, maybe 'cause there's so many of us.

There is a Snake Hill. Mamère says that one must be named for the mill owners or the landlords or the superintendents. My father don't laugh like the rest of us when she says things like that. He sits back and lets her do the talking. But later, through the wall, I hear his low steady voice warning her to watch her tongue.

3

A KNOCKING AT THE DOOR

"Nosy old Madame Boucher must have told French Johnny to follow me," I tell the family later. "That's how he found Arthur." I'm still feeling sick to my stomach about this. If it hadn't been for me, Arthur could be miles away by now.

"Where did he think he was going to run to?" Delia asks.

We are sitting around the supper table. Now Pépé has his soup bowl in his bed. He is dribbling bits of food across the blanket. We never bother to clean it up until he's finished.

"Massachusetts," I say. "Across the border."

"What was the stupid boy thinking?" Delia says. "Vermont and Massachusetts. It's all the same country."

"There's a border between Canada and America," I say.

Delia laughs. "Borders between the states don't count the same as borders between countries."

I shrug, pretend I knew that all along.

My father snorts. "There are mills all over the place down there. Minute they see Arthur wandering the roads, they'll put him right to work."

Arthur might know how to read big books, but suddenly I think he's not so smart about other things. Like getting along in Massachusetts all by himself.

"He's a lazy one," says Mamère, sitting down. "He should have gone in last year, soon as his father died. Boy needs a firm hand."

"Miss Lesley says he's so smart he could be a lawyer or a doctor."

"That Miss Lesley," my mother says. "People got—"

I cut her off. "Miss Lesley says I'm one of her best readers."

"Don't be rude to Mamère," Pépé barks at me from his bed.

"Pardon," I say, but I use English. For Pépé, that's rude too. He gives me a look, but I pretend not to see.

"Good thing Arthur will be doffing for his mother," says Delia. "Mrs. Trottier's machine is down more than it's running."

"I told her today Delia won't be standing in for her no more." Mamère smiles at my older sister.

"I'm getting my own frames next week," says Delia. "Monday." She's all puffed up with herself.

"That means, *mademoiselle*, that soon as school lets out, you'll be doffing for me," Mamère says, pointing her wooden spoon at me.

"I can start now," I say proudly. "Tomorrow even."

Everybody looks at me.

"Grace got put out of school," says Henry. I kick him under the table. I wanted to be the one to tell them.

"Perfect," says Mamère. She's looking right at me. "Just when I need you."

My heart beats fast. Imagine Mamère needing me as much as she needs Delia.

"With Grace working, we'll have two and a half more dollars a week," says Papa, excited. Ever since he got sick, we've been trying to catch up. Even with Mamère and Delia working full-time and Papa in the picking room now, it seems the store bill gobbles up all the money. "Not right away, of course," Papa adds. "She's got to be trained."

"I know how to doff," I say. Well, I almost know. From standing next to Delia summers when I carry in the dinner pails.

Everybody starts talking at the same time.

"You're a quick one, Grace," my mother says. "You'll pick it up fast. We'll have to take in your papers. Tomorrow we'll go see French Johnny first thing."

I nod. You can't work in the mill till you're fourteen and I'm only twelve and two months. But Mamère knows how to get the right papers.

"I'll be making four and a half now," Delia says.

"We can pay off the bill at the store," says my father.

"Did you hear that, *mon père?*" Mamère yells with her face close to his beard. "Meat in your pea soup. Grace is coming into the mill."

"*Mon petit oiseau*, she is going home with me," Pépé says. "This summer."

Nobody pays him mind.

I jump to my feet and trot around the table. "Grace in the mill, money in the till," I call, patting first Henry on the head, then Delia, then Papa. "Grace to doff and spin, money in the bin." Pat on Mamère's head even though she tries to duck when she sees me coming. The others all begin to laugh and then Mamère gives that funny snort that means I've even gotten her going. I dance up to Pépé and pick up his hands and swing them back and forth as if we're turning round the room in a waltz.

Papa tunes up his accordion and Mamère begins to sing "*Si J'avais Ma Fronde*," which means "If I Had a Slingshot."

My father taps the beat with his foot and draws the sound out of the black bellows with one hand, while his fingers play the little keyboard on the side. My mother's voice skips along right behind. They don't take their eyes off each other for the whole song. The music always changes them. They look as if they've been glued together.

They met back in Canada when my father was hired to play and call a dance. Papa told us my mother stood in the front row for the first *chanson à répondre* and after that, he couldn't look at anybody else. She always says "Hush up" when he tells that story, but she don't mean it.

They start up a second tune about a growling old woman that reminds me of Madame Boucher. Delia grabs Henry for a dance and I jump up on the table and stomp my bare feet on the bare wood. The dishes are knocking about and Mamère waves at me to get down, but she is laughing all the same. Pépé is keeping time with his wooden spoon, *tik-tok*king it against the wall.

When the banging starts, I'm sure it's Madame Boucher upstairs telling us to quiet down.

But no—somebody is knocking at the door. The accordion sighs into silence and Mamère stops in the middle of a verse.

"*Entrez,*" my father says.

It's Miss Lesley.

"I hope I'm not interrupting." She's standing just inside the open door.

My mother's face is flushed red and she pats a thread of her brown hair back into place. "Come in," she says, but she looks as if she means go away.

I hop quick off the table and back into the shadow of the stove, next to Pépé's bed.

"I heard the music," says Miss Lesley, stepping inside. "I should have known Grace came from a dancing family. Her feet are never still."

Nobody says a word. That makes Miss Lesley fiddle with the fringe on the shawl around her shoulders.

"Mr. and Mrs. Forcier, you have heard that Grace left school today?"

I didn't leave. You run me out the door.

"Yes, that's fine with us," says my father. "Her mother needs a new doffer."

"Grace tells me Delia will be getting her own frames soon," says Miss Lesley. She is picking up each word and

26

putting it down in its own special place, the way she does with the pens on that high desk she stands behind in the schoolroom.

Delia was never no good at school. She couldn't wait to get out of there and Miss Lesley remembers that.

"Monday," says Delia proudly.

"Grace will doff for me," says Mamère.

"Grace is a good student," says Miss Lesley. "It will be a shame to lose her."

"You told me to go," I cry out, and they all turn to stare at me.

Miss Lesley is the first to look away. "I was hasty. I want you to let her stay in school longer, Madame Forcier."

The word *madame* is part of her begging. She is begging to keep me. Suddenly Mamère and Miss Lesley are fighting over me.

"Why don't I cut myself in two?" I ask. "Half of me for the mill and half for school."

Nobody laughs. Delia waves at me to hush.

With one long step, my mother is suddenly standing right next to my teacher. Miss Lesley shrinks a little.

"You were kind to come for a visit, Mademoiselle Lesley," my mother says in a big voice with her heavy accent. The word *mademoiselle* is part of my mother saying no.

She rests a hand on Miss Lesley's shoulder where the shawl is slipping sideways. She ain't exactly pushing, but they move together toward the door. "Another time we will offer you coffee, but the morning mill bell will ring soon enough, won't it?"

Just for a moment Miss Lesley seems the tougher, when she plants both her feet. "You will regret this. The girl could do so much more with her life."

"Yes, there will be time for that, I'm sure," says my mother, her voice tight. "But first we have to eat. And buy shoes and another blanket. And fatten up my father so he don't sicken again next winter. You understand." It is an order. If you do not understand, you should.

The door opens and closes and Miss Lesley is gone from our French Hill kitchen like a piece of dust blown out by the wind. I wonder if maybe I dreamed her there.

THE STORY OF THE COTTON

After Miss Lesley leaves, we stand for a minute without speaking.

"I'm sure that's her first visit to French Hill," my father says with a chuckle.

Mamère looks at the rest of us as if she's coming out of a daze. Then she snaps to attention.

"Delia," she says, "do Grace's hair so it's ready in the morning. Find her your old smock. Henry, clear the dishes and clean up your grandfather. I'll find Grace's papers. Tomorrow first thing, we'll go to see French Johnny."

Delia sits me on the bed. Every girl in the mill has to have her hair bound up so it don't get caught in the machines. Nobody's bothered with my hair since before Mass on Sunday so Delia's taking out five days of knots.

I try to pull away from her, but Delia's fingers are strong from three years in the mill. She holds tight.

I don't cry out. I don't ever let on that something hurts me. I'd rather drink my own blood.

"Be still, Grace," Delia says. "I'll tell you the story of the cotton."

I settle down.

She says, "Think about a cotton-picking girl smaller than you, dragging a bag behind her through the fields. She lives in the South. It's hot all the time. She snatches the cotton from the plants, one-hand snatch, two-hand snatch, step, one-hand, two-hand snatch, step."

"That sounds like Papa calling a dance," I say.

Delia straightens my head and starts the comb working through another clump of hair.

The cotton travels on the train from the Southern pickers to the Northern doffers. I close my eyes and imagine a long white rope stretching from that cotton-picking girl all the way to me.

"When the cotton gets here, the bales get opened," Delia goes on.

"That's what Pépé used to do. And Papa before he got moved up." For a whole year, Papa was loom fixer in the weaving room, but he got a weakness in his bones from moving in and out under the machines. One day they brought him home on a board 'cause his legs wouldn't hold him up no more. Mamère started in the spinning room that week to make up the extra money lost. She never come out.

It took Papa six weeks to get his legs to work right and by the time he was ready to work again, Mr. Wilson, the overseer, had given his own son the loom fixer job.

30

Everybody says the boy's lousy at it, nowhere near as good as Papa.

Delia's voice soothes while her fingers pull and straighten.

"The balers pick through the cotton just like I'm doing with this tangle of hair. The cotton's got leaves and grass and twigs caught up in it. And Southern bugs who took a big long trip on the train."

"I don't have bugs in my hair," I say, so she picks something out and shows me a beetle with a hard shiny shell, squirming between her fingers.

When she drops it on the floor, it skitters away. I would have squished it with my bare foot, but Delia lets living things live, no matter how small or squirmy. She's funny like that. And she still has me by my hair.

"It must have jumped on me today when I was down by the river looking for Arthur," I say.

Delia's voice starts up again.

"So the cotton goes to the carding room and the machine combs out the cotton the way I'm doing now. Takes a long time to make that cotton behave itself."

Finally the comb is traveling smoothly. I like the way the bone teeth scratch the itchy skin of my scalp.

Delia's talking again. "Then they send the cotton through the drawing frames to make those strands lie separate and flat, one next to another like your hair is doing now. They call it sliver." That's sliver like *driver*, not sliver like *river*. That's the chant Miss Lesley made up when she was teaching us our vowels.

Papa's working the drawing frames now. I put my hand back to feel, but Delia pushes it aside.

"The sliver gets stretched out and twisted into roving. The roving is wound onto big bobbins, stretched out again and wound onto even smaller bobbins," says Delia. Now the comb feels like a pencil drawing a line down the back of my head to split my hair in half. She divides those halves into threes to make the braids.

"The spinning machines twist that roving into thread," Delia says as she winds my hair around her fingers. "So we're the ones who turn it from fat cotton to thin thread. Then we send it down to the weavers, who weave thread into cloth."

Highest position Delia could ever get in the mill is weaving room supervisor. Delia wants it. Mamère says she's crazy to think that way. Most of the weavers are men and all of them are Irish.

"First the weft," Delia says, and my head jerks one way. "And then across it the warp." My head jerks the other.

She starts on the second braid. My head rolls back and forth between her hands, like a baby rocking in a cradle.

"Now you'll be the one doffing for Mamère, Grace," Delia says.

"I know that." Does she think I'm stupid?

"Don't mind her too much."

I keep my body still. Delia's telling me mill secrets. Her voice is low and solemn. If I turn around and look at her, she'll stop talking.

"She gets angry a lot. You'll make mistakes. Bound to happen. When you let those threads break and the machine goes on the loose pulley—"

32

She don't finish the sentence.

"Her pay goes down too," I say.

"That's right."

"And it will be my fault."

"Right again," Delia says. She don't speak for a while. Maybe she's thinking of the times Mamère got angry with her. "But she can be funny too," Delia says quickly. "She sings. And the women act like *she's* their boss, not French Johnny."

Delia turns me loose.

"What do you mean?"

She grins and starts up a game we played when I was little. She takes someone's part and then I have to make up an answer. "Well, excuse me, Madame Forcier, but may I please take my break over in the weaving room so's that Cordeau boy can see how shiny my hair is this morning?"

"I don't believe so, Mademoiselle Senay," I say in my best Mamère voice. "If you think I'll agree to that silly idea, then all that cotton you've been spinning must have woven itself right into your brain."

Delia's smile comes, but it goes just as quick.

"Are you girls fooling around in there?" calls Mamère.

"Yes, Mamère," I answer just as Delia puts her finger to her lips.

"Stop it," she hisses. "Don't get her fussing at us tonight. It's bad enough all day long."

We wait, but Mamère don't bother to answer my nonsense.

I liked having my sister hold on to me for that time. With Delia holding you, you wouldn't blow away like a speck of lint.

I run my fingers down the bumpy road of my braid.

She slaps my hand away. "Stop messing. That should hold for the night. Won't take me two seconds to pin it up in the morning."

Which is good, I think, 'cause two seconds is just about all we got in the morning before the mill bell starts to ring.

That night in bed with Henry tucked in between me and Delia, I think about Miss Lesley. She climbed up French Hill to get me back in school.

And we was all dancing and laughing and Mamère started singing again just 'cause I'm going into the mill.

But then I remember what Delia said about our mother in the spinning room and a little shiver runs round my skin.

I hear Pépé snoring in the kitchen. And then loud and clear right on the other side of the wall from my head, I hear my mother say, "It must be in the trunk."

We keep the important things in Pépé's trunk, the one he dragged up the hill from the train. The Bible, the tiny painting of Grand-mère by a wandering peddler who come through Rivière-du-Loup, the deed to Pépé's land, the rosary, my first Communion card.

If we ever have to leave in a hurry, that trunk is always packed, ready to go.

"Come to bed, Adeline," says my father's voice. "We'll look again in the morning."

"No time tomorrow," she says. More banging around. Then I hear her call, "Found it."

I'll never fall asleep, I think, but the next thing I know Delia is pinning up my braids when I'm only half-awake.

She drops her old mill smock over my head.

"Remember today—right for waste," she says, putting that hand in the empty pocket. She tucks a kerchief in my left hand and shoves it into the other one. "Left for lint. That's to remind you to clear the cotton from your nose and throat. Don't mix them up or you'll be sorry."

She leans down to look into my face. "Grace, every second. Pay attention."

5

MY PAPERS

I've been in the mill lots of times.

Summers ever since I was nine, I've been cooking the hot meal for Mamère and Papa and Delia and taking in the dinner pails in the middle of the day. Delia let me push her bobbin dolly. I played mumblety-peg or roll the bobbin with Dougie and Bridget and Felix when he was a summer sweeper boy in the spinning room. And grease skating. That's the best. Thomas invented that game. Too bad he can't play it no more with his twisted foot.

With all the oil dripping off the machines, bare feet slide around easy. The boys draw a line at the end of one alley, between the frames where French Johnny can't see us, and we run and set our legs into a long slide. I'm skinny for my age and I've got big feet, but I can go the farthest 'cause I know how to keep myself low to the floor. Sometimes you slip and fall. That's a chance you take.

But now I'm here to work, not play.

The air in the mill is stuffy and linty and sweaty at the same time 'cause all day long water sprays down on the frames from little hoses in the ceiling. Wet keeps the threads from breaking. The windows are shut tight even in the summer. You don't breathe too deep for fear of what you might be sucking down your throat.

People complain about the noise, but it's not so bad in the spinning room. The belts up above our heads slap and the big roll drives turn and the bobbins spin like a thousand bees buzzing. You get used to it so you almost miss it when you step outside. The world seems too quiet all of a sudden.

The weaving room is the worst. In there you get a pounding sound every time a beam slaps into place. And there are a hundred beams slapping at once and the whole floor shakes and jumps. Most of the people who work in weaving go deaf early on. That's why I say Delia should stay in the spinning room even if she won't make as much money.

You're not supposed to work in the mill until you're fourteen, but visiting is fine. French Johnny likes us kids going in and out all the time. He says, that way we get used to the work.

The only people you worry about are the state inspectors. When French Johnny blows the whistle, all the kids in the mill, even the ones just visiting, know to run as fast as we can so he can hide us in the elevator that carries the cotton between the floors. The inspector always stops in at the front office and dawdles around there for a while so us kids have time to hide. Seems to me he don't really want to find us. We skitter across the room like those big cockroaches that come up through the floorboards in the summertime. Our mothers make a wall out of themselves to hide us.

It gets hot in that old elevator and the inspector can take hours to look through the mill, top to bottom. A couple of kids fainted last August and French Johnny had to throw cold water on them when he slid open the metal doors.

I didn't feel so good myself, but I didn't say a word.

"You look kind of green," Pierre Gagnon said to me when we filed out.

"Green Grace, green Grace," Felix shouted, and everybody called me that for a while. When nobody was looking, I smacked Felix hard on the top of his head. By the time he turned around I was gone. I've got fast feet, fast hands and fast fingers.

Now I'm really going to need them.

⌒

French Johnny is the first Franco second hand we ever had in the mill. Mr. Wilson, the overseer, is an English man from England and he wrinkles up his nose whenever French Johnny is near like he might catch something bad from him. Mamère says Mr. Wilson wanted another one of his sons to get the job as second hand, but the boy hated the mill so much, he run off and joined the army. Nobody else around who could do the job so the superintendent told Mr. Wilson he had to hire the Frenchman.

French Johnny don't have an office, but he has a corner

of the spinning room and even though it's got no walls, we all know not to go near there unless we're invited.

When he sees Mamère waiting with me, he finishes fastening on his white apron and straightens that bow tie. It looks kind of puny flopping around next to French Johnny's big thick neck, but he's proud to wear it 'cause then everybody knows he's second hand, even strangers coming into the mill. When he's done making us wait, he nods for us to take two steps into his area.

"My girl is here to doff," Mamère says.

"Got her papers?"

"Of course," says my mother, and hands him a piece of paper with some kind of seal on it. I stand on my tiptoes to look. It must have been hidden at the very bottom of the trunk.

French Johnny takes a long time. He reads pretty slow. "Says her name is Claire."

"Grace is her middle name. Claire after her grandmother."

Claire, I'm wondering. "Mamère, I never—"

My mother steps on my foot and goes on smiling up at French Johnny. He grins.

"Your girl is a talker. Just ask Arthur," he says with a nod over his shoulder at Mrs. Trottier's frame.

"Don't I know," says my mother. She lifts her boot to test if I'm going to keep quiet now. My bare toes are throbbing.

"I didn't tell you where Arthur was hiding," I blurt out, and down comes the boot. I yelp.

"Hope she's as quick with her fingers as she is with her mouth," says French Johnny. He's looking right at my mother.

"Look how Delia's done," says Mamère. "Forcier women are born to spin."

"And sing?" he asks.

Mamère shrugs, but her eyes sparkle.

In the space between them, I can see Arthur piecing up ends as fast as he can. But he's too late. A scavenger roll's already clattered to the floor, which means his threads are breaking all up and down the frame. They're going to have to shut down the machine to clean up the mess.

Even before he turns around, French Johnny knows what's happened. His ears are always cocked to the frames. When one of them goes down, it might as well be one of his children crying out for something.

"Two weeks' learner's pay starting today," he calls back over his shoulder as he goes to check Mrs. Trottier's frame.

I'm going to work. Right now.

"Arthur's got slow fingers," says Mamère. "Must run in the family. No wonder they only cover the two frames."

She is walking me toward her own six. Delia's already starting them up.

"Mamère, who's Claire?" I shout.

Mamère knows how to tilt her head and pitch her voice so I can hear her above the hum and buzz of the spindles. "The baby girl that died."

I feel a jolt in my stomach.

"When?"

"Fourteen years ago."

40

"You never told me."

She shrugs. "You don't count on keeping your children till they turn ten. No point. My mother lost four."

"What did the baby die from?"

"Fever. Never knew the cause. Little poorly thing right from the beginning. No use crying about that."

She says all this while marching across the spinning floor, waving at one person, then speaking in another's ear as we pass, making her hoot with laughter. All the spinners lift their heads when Mamère goes by except for Arthur's mother. She don't dare lift her head for nothing now that French Johnny has gotten that machine of hers up and running again. Won't be long before her other one goes down.

I trot along behind thinking about all those years when Mamère wasn't counting on me living past the age of ten. It's too big and strange an idea to take in. I decide it can't be true. She must have known I was tougher than that sickly older sister of mine.

Then I have no time to think about anything but bobbins.

6

DOFFING

"Stand still, Grace."

Delia sounds like Miss Lesley. Why is everybody always telling me the same thing?

"I'm not doing nothing wrong."

"Keep your smock away from that frame. You need to mind so you do this right."

"I already know what to do. You don't have to show me."

We are shouting at each other even louder than you need to in the spinning room. She won't let me touch nothing.

"How am I supposed to know how to do it if you keep pushing me aside?"

"By watching," she says, smacking my fingers when they get close. "Listen to me. Mamère runs six frames. Twelve sides. One hundred and thirty-six bobbins per side. That will keep your feet dancing, girl. We start them up one after another and each frame needs to be doffed at least once a shift." She nods up at a board posted on the far wall. "That's the schedule but Mamère pays it no mind. She doffs when she's ready."

I knew the frames were big. If you could take one of those frames home, it would stretch from our front door right through the kitchen over the garden to the outhouse in the back corner of the yard. Twelve times one hundred and thirty-six bobbins. I can't even count that high, but my hands are going to touch every one of them wooden babies I don't know how many times in a day. First when they've got fat cotton bellies and second when they're skinny and naked. The thought of my little bobbin babies gets me to giggling, which makes Delia cuff my head.

"Why'd you do that?"

"Grace, are you watching?"

I'm trying.

All the time she's talking and the frame is still running, Delia is unhooking a long wooden roll and guiding it out from between the spinning yarns. "Right now I'm clearing the scavenger rolls of lint, but you won't be doing this, you hear, Grace? This is Mamère's work and you better not mess with it. She's only now making me do it 'cause I'm practicing for my own frames."

"You better not mess with it," I repeat in that Delia voice that thinks it knows everything. I burst out laughing at the prissy pinched look on her face.

"Grace," she spits, her face up close to mine. "Stop with your fooling. Right now."

I stop.

43

Delia feeds that wooden scavenger roll back in between the running ends. Everything is moving so fast that I can't make my eyes stay on the part they need to look at. All I know is if Delia moves that roll one little inch out of line, she'll slice through a bunch of ends and we'll have a mess on our hands.

When I see her stuffing the waste in the pocket of her smock I start up my little chant. Right for waste, left for lint. I need to keep that straight.

"Doff number one," Mamère yells. We run. Mamère lowers the ring rails with her foot pedal and throws the shipper handle on the top so the whole frame shuts down. Delia scoops up four empty bobbins from the cart pressed against her hip.

I can barely follow the movements as she lifts the full bobbin off with her left hand, drops it in the box on the top of the dolly and lowers the empty bobbin over the spindle with her right hand. Her eye seems to guide her to the tip of each spindle. Her hands move as quick and regular as the machines. Step to the left, bump the bobbin dolly, lift, drop, lift, drop, lift, drop, three more done. And all the time Mamère is watching her other frames, but you can feel her waiting to start this one up again.

I take three empty bobbins from the box to practice holding them in one hand, but they slip away from me. Two hit the floor. I wipe them off with the bottom edge of my smock.

"Your hands aren't big enough yet, Grace," Delia calls to me without shifting her eyes off the frame. "Start with one bobbin at a time. It takes practice. Hold the empty one with your right hand because we're moving to the left. Doff with your left, replace with your right. You don't want your hands crossing one over the other. It will slow you up too much."

I try doing what she says, but my right hand feels lumpy and useless. I always do everything with my left hand. Mamère says that left-handed people are touched by the lucky stick. But I don't feel lucky right now when I've got to learn this big bumbling right hand to hold the empty bobbins.

At the end of the frame, Delia dumps her waste. Then we turn the corner and come back down the other side, another one hundred and thirty-six bobbins.

"Ready?" Mamère calls. Her voice sounds peevish. She has already reset the builder, that green metal wheel in the corner of the frame. She has to crouch down to do it, which is why the hem of her skirt is always black with the oil from the floor.

"Almost," Delia calls back, and she speeds up so her hands are flying through the air like birds. Last bobbin slides down over its spindle. She nods to my mother, who throws the shipper handle to start the frame up again.

"All the ends are slack now," Delia says into my ear. "Watch while she jogs the rail." Mamère taps the foot pedal once, two times, three. "That gets the snarls out. Now pray all the ends are up." The frame starts its whirring, spinning work again and I start breathing too even though I didn't know I'd stopped.

45

On our way down the row, Delia pulls up suddenly to twist together two broken ends. I run smack bang into the back of her so hard I almost knock us both over. She spits out my name as if it's a bad taste and I scrabble away to give her room.

From down the row Mamère calls, "Doff number two," and Delia's hands start flying again and I'm watching so hard that my eyes could burn holes in the thread.

———

By midday break my entire body is vibrating from trying to learn everything at once. The women gather in one corner of the spinning room to eat with us doffers passing in and out of their circle.

It feels like I've got to clear the lint out of my throat before my dinner can make its way down so I stand to the side, hawking and spitting into the handkerchief. Soon my mouth burns raw from working so hard.

"Don't bother," Dougie's older sister Bridget tells me. "Your food will taste like the cotton no matter what you do."

I settle myself near Arthur. I can't tell which is shaking harder, my body or the floor we're sitting on. In the weave room above our heads, the seven hundred looms with their slapping shuttles march along in regular time just like an army on the move. Up there, they take their break in shifts so the looms never shut down.

"You reading the book about the soldier boy?" I ask Arthur.

Bridget shoves him with her elbow. "Girl spoke to you," she teases.

"Best not talk to her," Arthur says in a loud voice so everybody can hear. "That Grace is a tattler. She's dangerous to have around."

"I am not," I say, but he don't speak again. He's got his book in one hand and his cold sausage in the other. When I lean way over to see the name of the book, he buries it deep in his lap.

I get up and move away.

Bet it is the one about the soldier boy. Bet Miss Lesley didn't make him give it back. I wonder what book Thomas and Norma and Rose and the rest are reading in school today. It must take them a whole day to get through a page with the two best readers gone.

Suddenly I miss the feeling of all of us in that room together with the little kids droning away in the front rows and the sun sliding in the open windows and the cough and grumble of the river running over the rocks down at the bottom of the hill. Here with the dirty streaked windows shut tight, it seems like the school and French Hill and Pépé and Henry all disappeared. It gives me a queer lost feeling.

I jump up. "Let's play a game," I say. The others are waiting for me to start something so I hop over to a long skinny pipe lying in the corner.

"Follow the leader," I call, and with my hands out for balance, I walk the length of it, my bare feet curling around the cool metal.

Nobody moves. "Come on," I shout, and do it again, quicker this time. Two of the boys follow and then Bridget tries and slips off twice.

"Take off your shoes, it's easier," I tell her.

By the time she's got it right, I've gathered up a pile of waste and packed it into a greasy lint ball. I toss it Arthur's way, but he just pulls to the left so it floats by. Hubert, a bobbin boy, picks it up and tosses it back at me. Now all the kids are scavenging for the biggest lint balls and rolling them in the grease. We're having a great cotton ball fight when Mamère hoists herself up on the high windowsill and calls, "Grace, enough nonsense," and we have to stop.

Sitting up there, Mamère looks like the queen of the spinning room. She tells Mrs. Senay what to do about her ailing baby and asks Mrs. Cordeau when Norma will be coming in. You can tell from the way she says it that she thinks Norma should have started in the mill a long time ago. Big girl like that.

"Grace is going to be a quick learner just like my Delia," she says to nobody in particular. I keep my head down. I'm practicing picking up and dropping a bobbin with my right hand. I might as well be trying to lift it with my teeth. What is wrong with that hand?

"Sing us a song, Adeline," calls Mrs. Trottier. I'm surprised to hear her speak out. She's normally so quiet and frightened-looking. But I know she loves music. On Sundays, she plays the little organ the Congregational church passed on to us Francos when they got the money to buy a new one. Imagine having a brand-new organ. Or a

48

church that ain't just a room above a store, but a real church with a bell that rings as loud as the mill bell.

Père Alain says Mamère has a voice like an angel. He always puts her right up front at church to lead us in the singing of the Kyrie and the Agnus Dei.

"Give us *'Le Grain de Mil,'* " calls Mrs. Senay.

"Yes, Mamère," I cry. It's my favorite 'cause the beat is so strong it gets everybody's feet to dancing.

"Par derrière chez mon père, il y a un pommier doux," she starts. Behind my father's house there is a sweet apple tree. Her clear cool voice rises up to the rafters like a bird let loose.

Mrs. Trottier starts the clapping and Delia clacks two empty bobbins together to help her keep time. Soon enough everybody joins in the singing, following Mamère's lead. I grab Bridget and we turn in a circle, our arms linked. You can't hear the beat coming from my bare feet, but Bridget's stamping her shoes in time to Mamère's voice. The faster she sings, the faster we dance. I'm so happy all of a sudden. Here I am in the mill with my mother and sister and I'm part of the grown-up life they been living every day without me.

I'm so lost in my dancing that I don't hear the commotion until Bridget yanks my arm and I finally go still.

The trouble is coming from Arthur's corner. Boy must be deaf. He ain't moved the whole time Mamère was singing.

"Give it to me, boy," says Mr. Wilson. "You know the rules about reading in the mill. John," he shouts. His voice flies around the room. "Get over here."

Arthur is holding on to his book as if it's his own arm and Mr. Wilson is trying to snatch it away from him. French Johnny comes striding down the aisle between two frames.

Uh-oh, here's trouble. French Johnny made a deal with Arthur that he could read long as he didn't let the overseer catch him.

"This boy is reading," roars Mr. Wilson at French Johnny, as if he thinks Arthur just murdered someone. "It's against the rules. If you can't keep order in the spinning room, we'll have to find somebody else to take your place."

Mamère is watching with a smirk playing round her mouth. We all know Mr. Wilson don't have nobody else for second hand, but he throws this up in French Johnny's face often as he can.

"Take that book away from the boy," he demands.

"*Donnez-le-moi,*" French Johnny says in a low voice. He only uses our language when he really needs us to go along with him. It's a kind of signal. If Arthur gives the book up easily, there's a chance he might get it back again. But if he makes French Johnny look silly in front of the overseer, then he'll never see that book again. Or no other for that matter. And he won't be able to sit down on his backside no time soon either.

Arthur hands the book over.

"The boy needs to learn to speak English," says Mr. Wilson.

"He can read it well enough," says French Johnny, holding up the book. I jump up to see. *The Red Badge of Courage*. I was right. Delia pulls me down again. You don't want the overseer picking you out of the crowd.

Mr. Wilson ain't sure what to say to that so he stomps off without another word. French Johnny gives us all a look and his eyes come to rest on my mother. They seem to talk to each other through the air without speaking out loud.

"Cleaning time," says Mamère, pushing herself off the windowsill, and we get back to work.

7

ARTHUR SPEAKS TO ME

This is the day we get to quit two hours early, but first we shut the frames down for cleaning. All week long the lint floating around in the air comes to rest on the cotton roving and they stick together. Then the roving gets stubborn and won't feed properly onto the bobbins. That means by Saturday the ends are breaking on every machine. If you don't catch that first break and piece up by twisting the threads back together, sure thing there'll be another. It's a miracle only two ends broke after we doffed our first frame. On the second one, Mamère and Delia pieced up twelve between them. Every frame we doffed, it seemed more ends broke.

Mamère has a hook she uses to clean between the rollers. Up and down and round the spindle pins, that hook pokes and pulls out the balls of cotton that have gotten themselves messed up with the oil dripping down the gears. She throws the black squishy cotton balls on the floor for the sweeper boys to push away with their long-handled brooms. Delia is over cleaning the two frames she'll be starting up on Monday.

I don't have a hook so I poke my fingers in and around the secret little hiding places where it's too dangerous for them to go when the frame is running. In and out and in between I go, left hand and right, hunting for junk, snaking it out, flicking it away.

It's a dirty job, but for once it's quiet in the spinning room and you're not chasing bobbins. With nothing buzzing between you, you can talk to people easy-like when you spy their face on the other side of the frame.

Suddenly something snatches my smock and yanks it down. I jump back with a scream.

It's Arthur who reached under the frame. Stupid trick. Kids do it to tease each other all the time. We all know the machine can rip your clothes right off if you're not paying mind.

"I was just fooling you," he says. "The frame's not even running." He's standing up now. I see one half of his face between the mess of spindles and gears, then the other.

"Why don't you go clean your own frames?"

He shrugs. "It's more fun tormenting you," he says. He don't have too many friends, so I think this is his dumb way of getting back with me. "I like this part," he says. "So many places to fit my fingers." And I can see them poking through from his side. Arthur has thick fingers, better for cleaning than doffing.

"Papa will make me a hook next week," I say. "Want one?"

He shrugs. "Maybe."

53

"Let's try and touch," I say.

It's hard to find the exact right place where we will connect. First his fingers are too high and then mine are too far off to the side. It's like poking a needle through the back side of a shirt, searching for the hole in a button. In the end, it don't work anyway 'cause our fingers are too short. They just wave at each other in the dark space between the sides.

"Hello," I call.

"No talking, Grace," Mamère says from down the frame. "Work to be done."

I pull out a handful of gunked-up cotton balls so she can see I am working.

"Too bad about your book," I whisper to Arthur.

"He won't give it back. French Johnny don't like me."

"Bet I know where it is."

"How come?"

"I just know where he keeps his things." I know lots more about the mill than Arthur does. He never pays attention to nothing but his reading. "I can get your book back," I say before I think.

"Will you do it?" he asks.

"If you stop calling me tattle. It wasn't me who told French Johnny where to find you. It was Madame Boucher."

"But he followed you down the path. If it wasn't for you, I'd be gone by now. Across the border."

I shrug and move up to the next roller. I don't want to get his book back anyway. I don't even bother telling him how stupid he is about borders between the states.

You can't keep trying to be friends with a stubborn person like Arthur.

Suddenly there is his face again right across from me.

"Wonder what would happen if you put your fingers in here when the frames are running." He worms one chubby finger around the bottom of a spindle. Then he adds the second finger. There's no room to poke in a third.

"It would hurt you bad," I say. "It would gobble up your whole arm."

"Bet it would just hurt your fingers, maybe your hand a little."

"Why do that?" I ask. "That would be stupid."

"Maybe, maybe not."

Arthur is a strange one. I move again. My hands are full of grease now. The machines smell like a herd of old goats. I want to pinch my nose so I can get away from that smell, but then my fingers would carry the grease to my face. Wish there had been more to eat at dinnertime. My stomach is jumping over itself.

"All right," Arthur says. "I'll stop."

"You'll stop what?"

"I'll stop calling you names if you get my book back."

Why'd I promise that? I don't want to put myself on the wrong side of French Johnny. But I never go back on my word.

"One more thing," I say. "I want to know what's happening to the soldier. In the story."

"Deal."

"Deal." I swallow hard. How am I going to do this?

8

FRENCH JOHNNY AND MISS LESLEY

Soon as the bell rings I scoot down to the far end of the frame out of sight of my mother. She's busy anyway, helping Delia get her frames set for Monday morning. The new spinners are given the oldest frames in the room, the ones that make the most trouble. And they don't have doffers working for them. Delia will be running her legs off to keep up.

I stand over by the wall out of sight while the women stream past, hurrying toward the door. Most of the doffers are long gone already. Nobody wants to hang around the mill on a Saturday afternoon.

Arthur sees me hiding, but he don't let on.

"Where's Grace?" my mother asks him.

"She went on out," he says.

"Good girl," Mamère says. "She's picking up supplies from the store." My mother tucked a list in my pocket this morning. It is still there under my kerchief.

Once they pass out of sight, the spinning room goes quiet.

I didn't see French Johnny leave, but I don't hear him anywhere around. I skip along the back of the frames looking for him down each row but no sign. He must be talking to Mr. Wilson in his office on the floor below.

I sneak down to French Johnny's corner. His apron is hanging on a hook, which means he's probably left. If I don't hurry up and get out, they'll lock the gates on me. Last place I want to spend the night is the spinning room, where I'm going to be living every waking hour from this day forward. That's the way Père Alain talks when he prays.

There it is. Sitting right up on the windowsill. French Johnny is no reader so he's got no reason to take it home with him.

My hand closes around the book. I can see the place where Arthur folded the corner with an oily finger just before French Johnny took it away. He's almost halfway through. I skip back to the last line I ever read in school. The part about the great affairs of the earth.

I start reading again. My eyes jump right over the big words 'cause stopping to puzzle on them makes you miss out on the story. The boy dreamed of battles. But he never really thought he'd be fighting himself. I dreamed of the mill too. I never thought it would come so quick.

Suddenly, I feel a step behind me and French Johnny's hand comes down heavy on my shoulder. Stupid me. I forgot how quickly and quietly he can move.

I try to twist away, but he holds me fast.

"What are you doing, girl?"

"Getting Arthur's book for him."

"Looks like you was reading it."

"I can read as good as him." Well, almost.

"Who says I want to give that boy his book?"

"He won't read in the mill again, he told me." It's only a little lie.

"I'm not sure of anything with him. Or you either. You don't come near my office without my permission, you hear?"

I nod. Some office, I think.

"You sing as good as your mother?"

Now what kind of question is that? "No."

"No, sir."

"No, sir."

"But you know how to dance."

"Everybody dances," I say.

"Not in the mill, they don't. I seen Delia training you and those feet of yours don't ever stop."

First Miss Lesley, then Delia, now French Johnny.

"Don't people got better things to do than watch my feet?" I ask.

He bursts out laughing. "You're a funny one. Go on, take the boy's book," he says, and squeezes my shoulder one more time with those big fingers of his. He's strong enough to crunch my bones in two if he had a mind. But I think he's trying to be nice. He's just a big clumsy bear of a man.

Soon as he lets go, I hug the book against my chest and run as fast as I can.

"You tell that boy he better not bring that book in here

again," he shouts, but I twist down the stairs and across the yard without answering him.

Arthur is waiting for me on the other side of the gates. "They'll be locking up soon," he calls. "Did you get it?"

I hold it up to show him, but I keep running, my bare feet picking their way as best they can between the stones.

"Give it here," he cries, starting up after me.

"Come 'n' get it," I yell back over my shoulder. I don't know why I'm fooling him, but suddenly I want the feel of the wind blowing past me. I want to brush away the weight of French Johnny's hand on my shoulder and I want to get in all the running I can now I got the chance.

Arthur don't run as well as I do. He don't get much practice at it. I lead him down along the road to the railroad tracks, dodging a wagon delivering flour to the store and a crowd of younger kids. They turn right around and start chasing me too. My feet are getting tired, but I'm not letting them catch me now.

In one jump I'm across the southbound tracks, and then I stop 'cause the shake and rattle is coming up through my feet first and then the hot metal breath of the engine is blowing on me and Arthur shouting behind to go, go and I jump over the second set of tracks. The sudden whistling screech of the train knocks me off my feet and down the gravelly slope on the other side.

Then just as quick it seems the train is rattling away again and they're all around me, Arthur and the kids.

"Is she hurt?" someone calls in a low voice from the back of the crowd.

"I think she's dead," says someone else.

I could be, I guess.

"Just like Mr. Dupree's brother," says Dougie. He leans in. His nasty mouth is so close his spit sprays my cheek. "You dead?"

I'm not. My heart is hammering inside. I pretend to be taking my time while they all stand in a huddle, looking for blood. Then with no warning, I roll away and take off again 'cause I don't want them to see how scared I am and how close it was. I hear their cries right behind. They are spitting mad now. But somehow my legs keep on carrying me.

I duck down the side path by the school. The book is still high in the air above my head when somebody snatches it out of my hand. My feet shoot forward and I slide down on my backside. I get up slowly, rubbing the place on my leg where a sharp rock poked itself through my smock.

"Where do you think you're going with this?" asks Miss Lesley. She is standing on the front porch of the school, leafing through the book as if she just found it on the railing. I don't answer. I'm still catching my breath, waiting for my heart to stop making such a racket. "Can it be that Miss Grace has decided to be a reader instead of a mill rat?"

"It's mine," Arthur cries. "Grace stole it from me."

"I did not," I yell. "I stole it back for you. Arthur got caught reading in the mill. Besides, it's not your book anyway. It belongs to the school."

"In truth, it belongs to me," says Miss Lesley, still flipping the pages.

"Grace almost got hit by the train," Norma says. The others are gathered around now, half of them leaning over to catch their breath.

"Is that so, Grace?" Miss Lesley is staring at me now, the book slack in her hands.

I shrug. "I knew it was coming."

Her eyes dig into me so I have to look down quicker than I want to.

The rest of the kids start slinking away. Nobody wants to tangle with the teacher more than they have to. That leaves me and Arthur, glaring at each other. Funny. I almost got killed by a train, but he's the one who's still panting.

"Those trains are dangerous, Grace. And I told you not to take chances reading in the mill," she says to Arthur.

"I only do it during the breaks."

"Having the book in there distracts you," she says. "You have to pay attention to your work."

He shrugs.

When have they done all this talking together, I wonder.

"And how are you, Grace?"

"I'm fine," I say, but my voice sounds too loud for some reason.

"Delia's moved to her own frames?"

"Day after tomorrow."

"You on learner's pay for a month?"

"Two weeks, maybe more, depending."

Miss Lesley knows more about the mill than she lets on. "And I wonder what your mother used for papers. Bought them, I expect."

61

"She did not," I shout. "We had . . ." My voice runs out. I don't want to tell her about the sister who died fourteen years ago. Besides, Arthur is standing there listening.

"You had what?" she asks. Her voice is softer.

"I'm a fast learner," I say, turning my head away. "Soon I'll be able to doff quick as Delia."

"Using your left hand?"

When I wrote my letters for Miss Lesley, she made me switch hands. She said long as I wrote with my left hand, my words would lean the wrong way. With Miss Lesley there's always a right way and a wrong way to do things.

I told her she could tilt her head over to the side so my letters would look straight to her. I told her people and letters can't necessarily sit still or stand the way she wants them to.

"My right hand's in doffing school," I say smartly. Looks like her mouth starts to turn up a little, but she stops it just in time.

"At least you don't have to sit still anymore. I'm sure those frames keep you hopping." She snaps the book shut and hands it over my head to Arthur. "Tomorrow then?" she says. I turn around just in time to see him nod.

Then he's gone, ducked down the river path, and she's back inside the schoolroom with the door closed. I'm still standing there, but they've both slid away with no extra sound.

My legs start shaking something fierce. I sink down to the ground and sit there, my back against the wall of the school. Suddenly, the train is breathing down my neck again and I shut my eyes to push the picture away.

When I get home, Mamère is angry that I've forgotten to go to the store, but I only half hear what she is saying.

What are Arthur and Miss Lesley doing tomorrow, I wonder later when I'm sewing up the rip in my smock.

9

SUNDAY

Mass starts at nine a.m. sharp. Père Alain glares at you if you come in late. Mamère goes early to loosen up her singing voice. Delia makes sure that Henry and me are dressed proper.

My Sunday dress used to be Delia's. It's worn shiny in spots and I'm sick of its pattern and the bow at my neck, tighter now since I've been wearing it three years.

Henry puts on the Sunday shoes passed on by Madame Senay when Felix got too big for them. They've been worn by so many kids that the backs are broken down and no matter how much Pépé shines them, those old shoes make us look poor. Mamère hates that. One of the first things we're going to buy when we pay off the store bill is new shoes for Henry. That way he won't always be trying to hide behind me when we climb the stairs to the room above the store.

The mill owners charge us fifty dollars' rent a year for

this room. They like big Catholic families 'cause we give them lots of workers all in one package. There are so many of us now that anybody who comes late has to sit out on the landing and listen to Mass through the open door.

We are building our own church in this town, but so far, we've got nothing but one big hole that fills up with snow every winter. Nobody's making extra pennies to throw in the collection basket on Sundays. Even Père Alain has to chop wood for the farmers just to make enough money to feed himself.

Back in Canada, the people always collect themselves together on the steps after church and exchange news. Pépé told me that Sunday Mass was the only time you'd see your neighbors. Some of them had to drive two hours each way from their farms to get to church.

We still gather and talk even though now we're standing on the front porch of Mr. Dupree's store and it's spitting distance to our houses and to the mill, where we see each other every day. But this is the one time we can talk without the machines at our elbows.

Arthur is standing next to his mother. For once he don't have no book in his hand, but he looks restless. This is the to-morrow Miss Lesley was talking about and I want to know what the two of them are doing together. He may be her best reader, but I am the second best and that gives me rights.

Mamère's hand curls around my neck. "*Bonjour,* Grace," says Père Alain.

"*Bonjour, mon Père,*" I say, and drop into a curtsy. Mamère and the curé start in talking about the weather and Père Alain's sister, who's a nun in a little town right across the border in Massachusetts.

"Monsieur Cordeau is taking his uncle back to Rivière-du-Loup soon," says Père Alain. "And your father says he'll be going along too."

Mamère frowns. "Pépé's not right in his head," she says. "He's not sure where he is."

"And you started in the mill this week, Grace?"

"Yesterday, *mon Père.*"

"You work hard now. You'll be a great help to your family."

"Yes, *mon Père.*"

"And Delia has her own frames now," Mamère says. At the sound of her name, Delia walks over to join us.

I look around to see Mrs. Trottier standing in the same place as before at the edge of a group of women, but Arthur is gone. He must have slipped away when I wasn't looking. I twist out from under Mamère's hand and run to find him.

⏤

The schoolroom door is locked up tight, but when I tiptoe along the edge of the porch and peek in a window, I can see the two of them. Arthur's sitting where he always did right next to me, and Miss Lesley's in my old seat except her legs are stretched out straight and to the side 'cause her knees don't fit under our little desks. You can't move the

66

furniture around in the schoolroom. Each bench is screwed right into the desk behind it so nothing gets out of line. That's the way Miss Lesley likes things.

Funny. Only two days ago I was sitting there.

Their heads are bent so close together that Arthur's dark hair looks like it's growing right off Miss Lesley's head. I can't see what book they are reading.

This makes me mad. Why didn't she ask me to come? Why is Arthur so special?

Before I think too long about it, I'm banging on the window. They both look up with scared faces like I've caught them murdering someone. Miss Lesley marches over to the door. I hear her shoot the bolt across and I expect she's going to order me off the porch, but instead she yanks me inside the room and locks the door again.

"I didn't tell her where I was going," Arthur cries. "She followed me. She's always following me." All the time he's talking, he's shoving some paper into the cubby under our old desk. It's getting crumpled up. When his hand stops moving, a corner of it is still peeking out.

So they weren't reading. They were writing.

Miss Lesley hushes him. "You're turning into a first-class sneak, Miss Grace," she says in a quiet voice.

"Why won't you teach me on Sundays too?" I cry. I don't mean to say that. I don't mean to show either one of them that I care one little bit about the stupid old lessons they're having with themselves.

"You never asked me," Miss Lesley says, and her voice sounds surprised.

It's a wonder when you can shock a grown person. Of course, this time the words that popped out of my mouth surprised me too.

For once, I can't think what to say.

"Have you swallowed your voice?" Miss Lesley asks.

I shake my head, but still I don't say a thing.

"Arthur, shall we let her stay?"

He looks me up and down like I'm some kind of farm animal they're selling at the county fair.

"She'll just keep coming back if we don't. She don't give up."

He's right. I don't.

"You've got a secret, don't you?" I ask. And no matter what they say to me, I know I'm right. "What are you hiding?"

Miss Lesley puts both hands on my shoulders and steers me around so I'm sitting in my old place. It feels funny. Me and Arthur back in school. Except Miss Lesley ain't teaching us exactly. She's resting herself on top of the next-door desk where Norma and Rose usually sit. Now the three of us are all together like we're plotting something big.

And it turns out we are.

10

THE LETTER

Miss Lesley nods to Arthur and he pulls out the paper and smooths the wrinkles he made when he crunched it up.

"Read it to her," Miss Lesley says.

"Are you practicing your writing?" I ask.

"Grace, hush for once in your life and listen."

It's a letter. Arthur's doing the writing. It goes this way.

To Miss Anna Putnam, National Child Labor Committee, Vermont Chapter, Bennington, Vermont.

>*Dear Madam,*
>   *This is to inform you that there are underage children working in the cotton mill in the town of North Pownal, Vermont. These children range in age*

from eight to thirteen. They are em-
ployed in the following dangerous tasks.

It stops there.

"That's as far as we got," Arthur says. "Before you barged in."

"So now you can help us, Grace."

My brain is whirling around. My feet start shifting under the desk.

"What is that child labor comm—thing?"

"They investigate places where children are not supposed to be working because they are too young. Believe it or not, there are laws against child labor. They're just not enforced," Miss Lesley says.

"But we need to work. For the money." I can hear Mamère's voice speaking right through my lips.

"Yes, Grace. But you also need your education. Then when you get older, you'll have a job that makes you much more money than you'll ever get working in the mill."

"Stop arguing," Arthur says to me. "You wanna leave?"

I don't. This is more interesting than reading *La Justice* to Pépé for the third time this week. Or doing laundry with Mamère. Or weeding.

I'll help them write their dumb old letter. What difference does it make? When that inspector comes, we'll just hide in the elevator the way we always do until he leaves the premises. That's a fancy word Mr. Wilson uses for the mill.

"So back to the letter. What jobs do children do in the mill?"

"Doffing," I say.

"Besides doffing," says Miss Lesley.

"Sweeping," says Arthur. "And carrying the bobbin boxes. They're heavy."

"Good. Write that down. What else, Grace?"

I'm thinking hard. This is like a test and I want to do well on it. "Some of the boys work in the warping room."

Arthur writes.

"And what about Thomas?" Miss Lesley asks.

"He was fooling around at the time," I tell her. "He was standing too close to that gearbox."

"More accidents happen because of the number of children working in the mill. But Thomas was legally old enough to be working so we'll forget him for now. What else?"

"We clean the machines on Saturdays. And some other times if the roving gets too bunched up. Delia's got scars on her fingers from the cleaning hook."

"Perfect," says Miss Lesley, and I smile. I'm passing the test. "Arthur, put down machine maintenance." Then she writes out that big word for him so he can copy it.

"Why aren't you writing the letter to the committee place?" I ask Miss Lesley.

"She'll get fired if they find out it's coming from her," Arthur says, and rolls his eyes at me as if everybody is supposed to know that. "You'd better not tell."

"Who will fire her?"

"The mill owners," Arthur spits. "They own the mill school."

"Hush, Arthur," says Miss Lesley. "Nobody's going to be firing me as long as we keep this quiet. Now sign it this

71

way." She writes out another big word for him to copy. It says *Anonymous*.

"What does that mean?" I ask.

"It means the person writing the letter don't wish to be known," Arthur says. He acts like that's something he knew all along, but I bet Miss Lesley just told him that.

"Doesn't wish to be known," says Miss Lesley. She's always correcting our ways of speaking, but we don't remember from one time to the next.

She reads the letter over, folds it into an envelope and puts a stamp on it. "I'll mail this next week when I take the trolley down to Massachusetts to see my sister. That way nobody in this town will see it going out. Especially Mr. Dupree, the postmaster. He's the nosiest person in the town."

"Except for Madame Boucher," I say.

We sit awhile like we got nowhere to go.

"Arthur is staying for a lesson, Grace. You're welcome too if you want."

I do. We read a story in *Appleton's Reader* 'cause Arthur still has the soldier book. Miss Lesley directs me to read a poem called "The Brown Thrush" by Lucy Larcom.

When I start walking around so's I can read better, Miss Lesley opens her mouth to say something, but she shuts it again. Maybe 'cause this ain't real school she decides for once that it don't matter what my feet are doing.

When I'm done, she says, "Do you know who Miss Larcom was, Grace?"

I shake my head.

"She worked in the spinning room in a mill in Lowell,

Massachusetts, when she was your age. Fifty years ago. She ended up writing books. You could do that too. As long as you have an education."

"But you told me underage children don't have to work in Massachusetts," Arthur says to Miss Lesley.

"Not now. Massachusetts is one state that enforces their child labor laws. But back in the 1840s, girls like Lucy couldn't wait to get to the mills. They were running away from the drudgery of the farms."

"So that's why you were running away to Massachusetts," I blurt out to Arthur. "So they wouldn't put you in a mill."

"Of course. I'm not stupid."

I look back and forth from one to the other. Seems Miss Lesley and Arthur talk about everything. I wonder again about all this happening right under my nose without me knowing it. Maybe it started when Arthur's father died. Maybe Miss Lesley took his place even though she's a woman.

⌣

On the way up to French Hill, Arthur tells me the story of the soldier in his book.

"Henry's worried that he's going to run away when the battle starts."

"His name is Henry then. Just like I said when we started that book." This is a wonder to me, that I could guess the same name for the youth as the man who wrote the book did. Maybe it means I will be a writer like Miss

Lucy Larcom. Except I think the poem about the brown thrush was boring and too-easy reading for me.

"Stop interrupting," says Arthur. "The soldier is wishing he's back on the farm, milking the brindle cow."

"Is there fighting yet?"

"No. Any minute now."

"You tried to run away," I say.

"Maybe I won't need to now. If those child labor people come, they could shut down the mill."

My heart stops. "If they close the mill, we won't have jobs."

"There's other work to do. We can go back to the farm and milk the brindle cow," he says with a grin.

"That's what Pépé wants, but my mother says that farming is much worse than the mill. She hated it just like Miss Lucy Larcom and those other mill girls. She never got paid one penny for her work."

"Nothing is worse than the mill," says Arthur before he turns off into his own house.

They would never shut the mill, I tell myself. Not 'cause of a bunch of kids.

"Arthur," I yell. "What does brindle mean?"

But he don't hear me.

11

THE FRAMES

I name my machines to help me keep them straight. The ones that give me the most trouble are boys. Albert, Edwin and George. Albert's got just about everything wrong that can go wrong. Even Mamère has trouble with him, but the machine fixers don't have time for little adjustments here and there. Mamère says long as we keep an eye on Albert, fuss over him, then he'll keep on working for us. Just like a man, she says. That's where I got the idea to name the bad ones after boys.

Delia's got two nasty frames with troubles from top to bottom. Now French Johnny spends his time over there when he used to torment Mrs. Trottier. I see Mamère keeping an eye on Delia and sometimes if I'm taking too long with my doffing, she runs over to help. At break time, she lets everybody know that Delia's got the worst two frames in the room. With all the boasting Mamère's done about us two girls, she can see the women smiling to themselves when Delia's in trouble. They used to smile that same way over Mrs. Trottier.

I told Delia to name her worst frame Thomas 'cause they both are limpers with something crooked about them, but she said I've got a wicked devil streak in me. I don't mean to be nasty. I just tell the truth the way I see it.

My three girls do fine. Marie, Thérèse and Bernadette. I named them after saints so's they'll keep on behaving themselves. I wish my hands were machines too, especially the right one. I can hold two bobbins now but that's not enough. I'm working myself up to four, but no matter how fast I go, I can always feel Mamère waiting on me.

I have bad dreams about my slow self that make me start up shouting in the middle of the night. Delia rolls me over and tells me to hush up and sleep. Henry don't even budge on his side. Henry could nod off in the middle of the noisy weaving room if he had to. Most nights Delia makes him sleep between us so I don't wake her with my thrashing.

⁓

Those first weeks were the worst. So many things can go wrong, especially at the end of the day when my feet get to aching and shaking and my back feels like someone has rammed a steel rod right down the middle of it and I can't twist or turn without the bones complaining.

But now it's better. I talk to my hands and my machines to keep them all doing the right thing at the right time. It's the plan I come up with to hold my mind still so it don't go wandering off. You've got to pay attention in the mill or else those big old bad machines, they'll snatch at any loose piece hanging off a person and gobble it up. After all, it's their job to grab the roving and spin it into thread. It's my job to stay out of the way and make sure they're spinning cotton and not a hank of my hair or one of my fingers or a piece of my smock.

I'm like Miss Lesley now with her eye on us school-children outside in the yard during recess. "Now, Albert, you behave yourself this morning or I'll have to shut you down, put you in the back of the room with the girls." "Edwin, I don't like that smart look you're giving me. No recess for you today. You stay inside and work right through the break." For once I can talk all I want with nobody telling me to hush. Nobody cares, long as I get those bobbin babies moved in and out of their cradles.

The thinking is what gets me in trouble. A picture pops in my mind of a kid biting Miss Lesley's finger in two or snatching at her dress the way a frame does if you give it half a chance. The very idea makes me laugh and then my mind follows that funny picture and suddenly, in the middle of the side I just doffed, a piece of slub gets through, which makes one end fly around and hit the next one and the next. Before I know it, I've got a regular snowstorm of cotton and my mother's throwing the shipper handle and yelling at me again.

Arthur don't work as hard as me. His mother's only got two frames. There's times I catch him staring out the window so fierce you'd think his eyes would burn a hole right through the dirty glass. He's still dreaming about running away. Dinnertimes when we break, he keeps on with the story of the soldier named Henry.

In the first battle, he stood and fought and was proud of himself. But the second time the Confederate soldiers attacked, he ran away.

"Why'd he run that time?" I ask.

" 'Cause he says it's the duty of every little piece of the army to save itself," Arthur says.

"If everybody thought that way, there'd be no army left."

Arthur just shakes his head like I'm a crazy person.

—

Delia's machine is down again, third time since the starting bell.

My mother yells, "Doff number six," which is Thérèse and I'm already there tending to her.

"My good girl," I whisper to her as I scoop up my empty bobbins, nudging the bobbin truck along ahead of me. And my right hand is getting smarter. This is the first day it's been able to hold three bobbins at once. I drop each one cleanly over its spindle with no trouble. Thérèse's bobbins come off just as easy in my left hand. I'm humming now, clocking along as regular as my frame, the full bobbins piling up in the box on top of the bobbin truck. I flip the separators back in place and drop down the thread boards faster than ever before.

"Done," I yell, but Mamère don't hear me 'cause she's still fussing with Delia's frame. I look up at the board where the doffing schedule is posted. We're ahead on number six, but then like Delia said, my mother don't pay much attention to that schedule. I signal for Hubert the bobbin boy, and he comes along all bent over like he's running at a wall. He's so short and scrawny it's the only way he can get the big bobbin truck moving. Off it goes with Hubert's skinny legs and toes doing the pushing, his black oily heels never touching the floor.

Number one, Albert, is filling up so I figure I'll save time and clear his scavenger rolls. It's the spinner's job, but I've watched Mamère and Delia do it a hundred times. I pull over a box, step up on it and lift up the first roll with several laps of lint.

"Come on, Albert, you behave now. Easy does it," I whisper, and even though it's heavier than I thought, the roll is sliding out just the way it should.

"What are you doing?" shouts French Johnny's voice in my ear and I jump and sure enough, a lap hits an end soon as I take my eye off it and the broken end wraps around the bottom roll. By the time I work it out at least eight ends are down.

Mamère pushes me off the box and out of the way with one rough hand, throws the shipper handle with the other just as the next scavenger roll down the way spits itself out onto the floor. I stumble backward and my feet slip.

It's French Johnny who sets me right, one of his big hands curled around each of my shoulders, but I twist away from him soon as I get my balance.

The whole time my mother is screaming, *"Bête, bête, bête, stupide fille,"* and the way her voice is pitched everybody can hear and they look up as French Johnny walks away with a grin on his face.

Now we have at least twelve ends flying around on Albert, and my mother has to shut down two other frames so they don't spill over. I piece up, twisting the thread together fast as I can, but she's faster of course and soon as she catches up with me she just shoves me out of the way with her hip. I wipe down the scavenger roll and shove the wad of lint into the pocket of my smock, but she snatches the roll from me and clears it again, which is her way of saying nothing I do helps none. She can't count on me.

The pain in my chest comes from not breathing 'cause if I breathe I will cry and I don't never let myself do that.

———

At the dinner break, I sit by myself, hunched over my knees. Delia tries to get me to eat, but I shake my head. The pain in my chest has spread to my stomach. Whatever I swallow will come back up, I'm sure of it. Better to stay hungry.

I see Arthur heading over to my corner, but I give him a stare that makes him veer away.

I don't look at Mamère, but I can hear Mrs. Trottier talking to her.

"Don't be so hard on Grace. It's only her third week," she says, and I want to kill Arthur's mother, grind her up between my teeth and spit what's left of her little bony bones out the window. Last thing I need is that woman standing up for me.

I cringe waiting for Mamère's answer.

"You pay attention to your own business, madame," says my mother in a sharp voice. "I train my girls whatever way I please. They learn their jobs right. If Delia hadn't taken so much time piecing up your ends, she would have gotten her own frames months ago."

I peek through my fingers to see them glaring at each other, trembling like two dogs ready to fight. Mrs. Trottier backs away first and my mother smiles in a way that says, I won. She always wins her spats with people.

Only thing bigger and bossier than my mother in the spinning room is the frames.

When we walk out of the mill that evening, Arthur stays away from me. The soldier story usually takes my mind off my troubles, but I pretend I don't care to hear it tonight.

⌣

It is raining. I tip my head up so the water can run down my throat. Then I take the handkerchief out of my smock and press it to my mouth. Wrong pocket. I put that wad of scavenger roll lint in the wrong pocket and now it's stuck up against my nose. I want to throw the garbage ball of cotton over the border into Massachusetts, as far away from me as ever it can get, but I don't have the strength. I toss it into a nearby bush and for some strange reason that's when the

81

crying starts. I've been holding those tears down all day long, but it's no use trying to stop them now.

I lean over to hawk and spit in the bushes. People pass me by, barely noticing, thinking it's only the cotton coming back up the way it does for all of us.

NO SAUSAGE

When Delia sees me coming in the door, she has the sense to keep quiet. Just takes a rag and wipes my face down as if I'm a baby.

Pépé is humming tonight and that's not good. Whenever he starts singing, it means he's even more out of his head than usual.

"He was trying to drag the trunk out the kitchen door when I come home from school today," Henry reports as we sit down to dinner.

"Don't do no harm," Mamère says.

"Sausage!" Pépé demands. He is stabbing at the potatoes in his bowl, looking for meat. There ain't been none since we had to pay Madame Boucher extra to look in on him mornings. I'm still on learner's pay. Mamère's pay is down too 'cause of me. And Delia's not making up the difference with her two cranky machines. Even with me working, we've fallen farther behind on the store bill. Papa says Mr. Dupree is cheating us, but there's no way to prove that.

Mamère shakes her head at Pépé. "Eat up, *mon père*."

"Sausage," he cries again, and throws his wooden spoon across the room. It slaps up against the wall and crashes to the floor. The brown gravy water leaves a long drip mark.

Nobody speaks. Then Mamère nods to Henry to pick up the spoon. She pulls herself to her feet, takes it from him and heads over to the bed to feed Pépé. Before she can get to him, he throws the bowl. It hits my mother square in the chest and bounces off her onto the floor. Her arm rises up automatically the way it does when she's reaching for the shipper handle and before she can stop herself, it swings across and smacks my grandfather full in the face. The sound of her flat hand against Pépé's old cheekbones makes a noise in the room like a bullet.

Papa pulls Mamère away and goes to comfort my grandfather. Delia dabs at the gravy stains on my mother's skirts, but Mamère don't seem to notice. She is staring off at some distant place, swaying a little. I squat down to mop up the spilled soup.

"Maybe Pépé should go back to Canada," I say to myself. I'm so tired that my voice slurs around and I expect nobody is really listening in the commotion. "He would be happier then and we could be eating this food, not wiping it off the floor."

Mamère cuffs me on the top of my head and the blow is hard enough to snap my neck back. I go still.

"And maybe you could learn your job, *mademoiselle*, instead of thinking you're quick or smart enough to do mine.

And then we would have food to eat and shoes for your brother and all the sausage Pépé deserves."

Everything is my fault. I'm the slow doffer and the one who made Pépé throw his bowl, which made her slap him. I'm more trouble than I'm worth. Maybe that sickly sister of mine should have lived. Maybe she would have turned out better than me. A bubble of fury rises up inside me at the idea, but for once, I know enough to lock my lips together. Seems whenever I talk I get myself in trouble.

I squeeze the soup-gravy rag into the sink and slide back into my own chair. The soup is cold now and hard to swallow, but I force it down. If I don't eat, I won't sleep. And if I don't sleep, I won't doff no better in the morning.

After supper, Mamère kneels in front of Pépé before we gather for the rosary to ask his special forgiveness and his blessing. He looks at her out of his cold blue eyes and nods, but he don't speak.

Papa has to lead us in the rosary. Pépé's fingers move the beads, but he mumbles so low in his beard that we cannot tell whether he is praying or prattling nonsense again.

Later I hear my father say that we'll have to tie Pépé to his bed when we leave in the mornings. That way he can't go wandering off and we won't have to pay Mrs. Boucher. My mother don't answer. Or maybe she does and for once, her voice is so low that I can't hear it through the wall.

I remember the night Miss Lesley caught us dancing. How long ago that seems.

⌣

85

It takes me four whole weeks to come off learner's pay. Two longer than most kids. Some days go better than others, but I can't count on my fingers to behave. They don't hold the learning in them the way my brain can hang on to a word in a book. I wish I were a machine. Then there'd be a reason for my mistakes and the loom fixer could oil my roll drive or straighten my spindles and that would be the end of it.

Arthur tells me it's 'cause I'm too smart for the work. If it interested me, I could pay attention better. I don't say nothing to that, but I do know when I'm at the frame, it's easy for my mind to fly off just like an end that ain't piecing up proper. But Arthur is smart and he can think and doff at the same time. I can only do one or the other.

And no matter what, I cannot please Mamère. There's always an end I haven't caught or a bobbin I've dropped. Things people say get stuck in my head and I waste time fussing over them so I try to close my ears against her voice. She sees that and yells even louder. She don't care no more what the other women in the spinning room think of me 'cause she's given up on me herself. She's got one good daughter and one bad doffer.

"I told you she can be that way," Delia says to me at night when I'm lying stiff in the bed. "Don't pay no mind to it, Grace. It's her way of worrying."

"I don't care," I tell Delia, but the words don't come easy. It's always hard for me to tell a lie.

13

ROPES

We're trying to keep it a secret, but we're tying Pépé to the bed now. In the beginning, he batted Papa's hands away and spat at the ropes, but Mamère give him some mixture of herbs those first few days that made him quiet. Then he seemed to get used to it. Now he sleeps most of the time. Papa comes home at the dinner break to get him up and feed him something. If the weather is good, Papa sets him in the chair outside our front door for a while so Pépé can turn his face up to the sun.

We told Madame Boucher that Pépé is much better and we don't need her to look in no more. But Henry knows to lock the door when he leaves for school so the portly Madame don't poke her nose into our business anyway.

It ain't right for Pépé to be tied down like that. I remember him telling me how much he hated the work inside the mill 'cause he felt so cooped up.

One time the circus come through our town on its way south. It didn't stop 'cause there's no money to be made in a little postage stamp of a town where the mill workers put all their extra pennies in the church basket. But I remember seeing the lion curled up on his side, staring through the bars of his cage as it bumped along the main street of the town behind a wagon. His fur was matted and in some places, the bare skin showed through in patches. He didn't even move or lift his head when Dougie and Thomas threw pebbles at him.

Pépé used to be as strong as that lion and now he lies still and stares at the wall as if he can see right through it. I want the old Pépé to come back to us. When his eyes are open, they never blink. I still read *La Justice* to him Wednesday nights and I talk to him all the time when I'm home.

For once, Mamère don't hush me up. Maybe she's glad someone is talking to him. Ever since the night she slapped his face, it's hard for her to look at him.

I can't tell if he hears me. Sometimes he hums, sometimes he mumbles deep in his throat. But whenever I squeeze his hard bony hand, he squeezes back.

⸺

Sunday morning I wake up choking.

Delia shakes me. "What's wrong with you?"

"My throat is swollen shut," I croak. I was dreaming that all the lint I'd swallowed had come crawling back up from my stomach.

"Don't be stupid," says Delia. She puts a hand to my forehead and calls to Mamère that I have a fever.

Mamère is late for Mass already when she comes in to have a look at me. "You can stay home, Grace. The good Lord understands that we need you doffing tomorrow more than praying today." But she says this in a low voice so that my father don't hear. "You can let your Pépé up to sit in the sun. When he woke earlier, he was making sense. Just like his old self," she adds, talking more to the air than to me.

I nod and when she leaves, I let my pounding head fall back on the mattress. I sleep and wake again to a cry from Pépé.

He is struggling up, fighting the ropes, but when he sees me, he calms down.

"I'm here, Pépé," I say, taking his hand. "I'm here."

"I see you, *mon petit oiseau*," he says. He is speaking clearly and calling me his little bird again.

"You look well this morning," I say. My voice sounds thick.

"And you do not, my little Grace," he says. Maybe whatever sickness he had has passed to me.

"Delia says I have a fever," I tell him.

"Your hand is warm. Let me up."

"Are you strong enough, Pépé?" I ask.

He looks sternly at me. "Grace, I am your Pépé. Now, let me up. I will pick the root vegetables from the garden and make you a healing broth."

My old Pépé is back again. He will spoon warm soup between my lips and put a cold rag on my head to stop the pounding. The world has turned again so things are as they should be. I am just a girl sick with a fever, and he is my grandfather, the one who's always taken care of me.

89

My fingers are used to piecing up fine strands of cotton yarn. They struggle with the thick ropes. Then they stop.

"Pépé, it's June. Henry started the planting just two weeks ago. There are no vegetables in the garden yet."

He looks confused for a minute as if he's thinking this problem over. "June," he says. "Radish soup."

He used to make me radish soup when I was little. With the green radish tops dropped into the water at the last minute. My fingers start working through the knots again. Pépé is acting like his old self. Won't Mamère be happy?

His legs start to slip out from under him the first time he tries to stand. He puts a hand on my shoulder and I almost crumple under his full weight. He grabs the doorknob, straightens, sways, tests one foot, then the other.

"Stiff," he says. Then he turns to me. "Back to bed with you. I shall go out to pick the radishes."

This worries me. He ain't been outside in days and only then to sit on the chair in the sun with Papa watching him. "No, Pépé, I'll go to the garden. You boil the water."

He looks at me again, thinking through this new idea, and I almost laugh out loud at the pair of us. My throat stuffed as fat as an uncooked sausage and his old legs creaking their way around our kitchen while his brain tries to sort out my words. We're not much good for each other, are we? But Pépé is talking to me and making sense again. That's all I care about.

"You're right," he says. "You dig up the radishes and I shall boil the water for soup."

When I see he is able to lift the dipper from the pail

Henry brought in from the pump, I head out the back door to the garden.

He calls once more to me.

"Grace," he says, "tell your mother it's time for me to go. You give your mother that message. From me."

He's talking about Canada again. "But, Pépé, she'll be home from Mass soon," I say. "You can tell her yourself."

"Yes," he says, and he stares at me hard as if he's trying to hold on to the idea of who I am. "Get the radishes, then."

⁓

I'm dizzy myself, especially when I lift my head too quickly from rooting around in the ground. I think of all the days I've ached to be outside the mill, but this morning the sun on my back feels like a heavy package I have to carry. The radish plants way off in the north corner are puny-looking little things, but the greens will be good. On the way back down the row, I break off some early shoots of lettuce, one or two from each plant the way Pépé has always learned me. Two for eating, three for growing, he says.

When I don't see him by the stove, I think he must have gone to rest in the other room. I take care to pile our small store of June vegetables neatly on the kitchen table where he can reach them easily. Mamère will not like the mud on the tablecloth so I must remember to clean that off. I slump into the seat, everything aching from the short trip to the garden and back.

"Pépé, the radishes are small, but they'll do," I say, my head down on my hands.

He don't answer. How can he possibly hear me when my lips are pressed against the scratchy wooden planks of the table?

"Pépé," I say louder. "Is the water boiling?"

I stumble to my feet again. He's not resting in my room or on his bed in the corner. Pépé is not in the house.

Oh please, Pépé. Don't be gone away. Not now. Not when I am supposed to be watching you. Don't give Mamère no more reasons to be angry with me.

I remember it is June and it is a Sunday. Pépé always went fishing on summer Sundays. That's where he has gone, down to the river. I can bring him back before Mass lets out. I can have him tucked right into bed by the time they come up the hill.

If only my legs would move more quickly and that shuttle pounding away in my head would stop slapping back and forth.

14

THE TRAIN

My feet carry me across the empty road and down the path that winds around the schoolhouse. Nobody will be out and about until Mass is over. Please, Père Alain, I pray, please talk long today.

I slide into the woods, where it is cool and quiet. I ain't been down this way since the day I followed Arthur to the trapper's shack. I call Pépé's name, but my voice is feeble. It don't even stop the birds from their singing. My bare feet trip on the knotty brambles and I grab for a tree to steady myself, but I go down anyway. The damp ground cools my hot cheeks and I rest for a while, turning my face one way, then the other. It feels good not to move.

"I'm coming, Pépé," I call out, but he don't answer.

In the distance I hear the train coming north, hooting once, then twice like an owl. Then I don't hear no more after that.

Someone is carrying me.

"Pépé," I say. "We have to go back home now. We have to make the soup."

"Shhh," says the man's voice. My face is rubbing against his scratchy coat. I don't open my eyes.

Bells are ringing. Maybe they are inside my head as well.

"*Je l'ai trouvée*," shouts French Johnny's voice. Now I am sure I am hearing things. We bounce along, and he grunts like an animal as we climb a hill. Suddenly, we move out of the shade of the woods and the sun hits me full in the face. I am rolled out of his arms into another's.

"Grace," whispers my father, his breath a tickle in my ear. "*Merci à Dieu.*"

"Pépé is fishing," I say, my eyes open now. But my father's head is nothing but a black spot in the middle of the light. "I went down to the river to get him."

"*Fais dodo,*" he whispers in my ear. Is he ordering me to sleep or telling me a secret? I can't tell. "Close your eyes," he says. It *is* an order. I obey.

"French Johnny found her in the woods," he says when we enter the house. I feel the heat of many people moving about in our small kitchen, but still I keep my eyes closed. Papa will tell me when I can open them.

"My God, not her too," I hear my mother scream, and the room goes quiet.

"She is alive," says my father. "Burning with fever." He

won't let anybody take me away from him, and lowers me to the mattress himself.

I don't remember my father ever carrying me before. I feel lonely when he lets me go.

—

I am dreaming. Me and Pépé are walking along the river. I am carrying a bucket. Inside, the fish slide around on top of each other and their silver scales gleam in the sun. Then Pépé slips into the river and I call to him to come back. His head bobs along in the current and he is waving goodbye to me as he floats away. He is smiling.

"Are you going home to Canada?" I call. I am speaking English to Pépé and this is strange even in a dream.

"Yes," he answers. *"Grace à Dieu."* Thanks be to God.

That's what Grace means. Thanks be.

—

Someone is hushing me. I am so thirsty. Who is stuffing my mouth with cotton? I twist my head and spit again and push the hands away.

"Suck the rag," says the voice. It sounds like Madame Boucher, but when I open my eyes, nobody is there.

—

Next time I wake, Mamère is singing me a lullaby. *"Fais dodo,"* she sings. *"Fais dodo, mon petit oiseau."* I keep my eyes shut. I don't want her to see that I am listening. I don't want her to think I'm nothing but a poor, sickly thing that's going to die on her the way my sister Claire did.

⌣

Pépé is the one who's dead. He was hit trying to climb on the train when it was still moving. My father tells me the first morning that I can sit up.

I do not believe him. "Pépé is floating in the river," I say. My voice is still a croak. "He waved goodbye to me. He was going home to Rivière-du-Loup."

My father nods his head. "You are right, Grace. Pépé has gone home. But he won't be coming back."

I'm too weak to fight against the crying. Papa pulls me onto his lap and rocks back and forth in the chair, the way he rocks on his heels when he plays the accordion. It seems he don't mind holding me when we are alone. He never touches me in front of the others.

"Mamère told me I could untie him," I say at last.

"As I did many a time."

"But I left him alone when I went to pick the radishes."

"Your Pépé knew what he needed to do. He would have found a way to go no matter who had been with him."

⌣

Now my father is the one who says the rosary and gives the blessing. That night after supper, we gather in a circle around him. There are only five of us now.

96

"*Bon Dieu,*" he says with his eyes closed. "Thank you for giving our Grace back to us. And for gathering Pépé to your own sweet reward, the place where he suffers no more."

His voice sounds like music. It rises and falls like the bellows on his accordion. I've never really noticed that before. Pépé's voice was always the biggest in the house.

After the rosary, Papa rests his hands on each of our bowed heads and prays over us. Mamère is last. He puts his lips close to her ear and a shiver passes through her shoulders when she hears what he says.

"Mamère is quiet," I say to Delia that night. The bed feels big for the two of us. Henry is sleeping in the kitchen now.

"She can't forgive herself," says Delia to the air. "For slapping Pépé."

⌣

The next morning on the way to the mill, walking next to Mamère, I decide to tell her what Pépé said.

"Mamère."

"Mmm."

"Pépé said to give you a message."

She stops suddenly halfway down the hill to look at me. The other people part and move past us in the same easy way that the river flows around a rock.

"What did he say?"

I am trying hard to remember his exact words. " 'Tell your mother it's time for me to go.' Just that. I thought he was talking about Canada again. I said you'd be home from Mass soon and that he could tell you himself."

"Only me?"

She's testing me again. I take my time with my answer.

"Yes," I say at last. "The message was for you."

She's looking out over my head at something in the distance. We don't speak again.

———

I eat by myself. I can see the other kids thinking a death in the family is something you can catch as easy as a fever.

Arthur's the only one who comes near me. When he sits down, he says, "It's bad what happened to your Pépé."

"I don't want to talk about it," I say. I'm thinking if I don't talk about it then it didn't happen and Pépé is just visiting family in Canada. One day he'll come back. We'll pick the vegetables together and I won't rush so much. I'll wait for them to grow big enough.

But I don't mind Arthur being the one to sit next to me. He knows about losing people.

I lean over and spit through a crack in the floor. The glob is thick and flecked with lint. We both watch as it makes its way between the boards and disappears. Pity the worker down below.

"What's happening to the soldier?" I ask.

"Remember how he didn't run away from the first battle? But he did from the second. He figured out that he had to save himself. He done the right thing."

Then Arthur blurts out this long passage from the book

98

that he memorized. It's that same thing he told me before about every little piece rescuing itself.

"He said the rest of them be damned."

"Arthur, you shouldn't swear."

"I'm just quoting the book. So I'm going to save myself, Grace. You'll see. I'm figuring a way."

"Save yourself from what?"

"From the mill."

I shake my head 'cause I have no idea what he's talking about, but it must be the fever ain't left me yet.

I am slower doffing than usual. Mamère watches the hank clock, but she holds herself back from pushing me too hard.

Three days in a row she lets me off early and doffs the bobbins herself till the closing bell.

15

SCHOOL ON SUNDAYS

At suppertime now, Henry does most of the talking like our house is one big hole of silence he's got to fill up somehow with words. He tells us what's coming up in the garden, the news of the town, who's been smacked by Miss Lesley's ruler. The rest of us watch with hollow eyes and say nothing much.

Papa has started up smoking Pépé's pipe, but he never touches the accordion. Mamère has stopped humming. Delia spends hours down in the basement scrubbing the grease off the hem of her skirt. Night after night, Mamère sends me to fetch her.

Washing days we carry buckets of water across the yard from the pump and down the rotting wooden stairs. The basement's colder than ice in the winter, but summertimes it holds the cool in a good way. Baggy spiderwebs sway like hammocks from the rafters. You can hear muffled sounds through the floorboards from our kitchen, which is directly above.

The whole house has to do their washing in the two big laundry sinks so Madame Boucher assigns each tenant a washing time. We get Wednesday nights and Sunday afternoons.

Lately Delia's been living down there, it seems. If another family is using the big sinks, she just hunkers down in the corner, working out of the bucket.

"Come on, Delia, your supper's cold."

"I'm not finished."

"If it's grease you're getting out, you'll never be finished. There's always more."

She lets me lead her back upstairs and suddenly I feel like the older sister. I wonder some days if now she's the one with the fever. But it's not that. We are all of us looking for ways to hide from the ghost in the house. We keep hearing Pépé's voice and the rattle of his newspaper, keep seeing his thick fingers sliding around the circle of the black wooden rosary beads.

Henry sleeps in Pépé's bed now, except on the nights when we have boarders. The first man who came was a mill agent, sent by Mr. Wilson. He snored so loud the walls shook. Henry moved back in with me and Delia.

In the morning, the man was gone, leaving the slop jar full for me to wash out and his fifty-cent piece tucked under the sugar bowl. We used that money to pay down some of our bill at the store. Still, I hated the idea of that strange, smelly man in my Pépé's bed. Two more have come since. The second one complained at supper that there was no meat in his stew and the next morning, he left no money at all on the table.

Now Mamère knows to collect the board money first thing before she serves the evening meal.

—

The days after a bad sleep, the bobbins won't sit right in their cradles and the clearing board reaches out and snatches at every thread. Sometimes, I feel as if the cotton has filled my head and blocked my ears against most things, except Mamère's words. They slip past no matter what.

I'm not fast enough. Or I'm ahead of myself. Or I'm thinking I can do her job. Or I was born with clumsy fingers. Or I dream too much. Or my hands aren't quick like Delia's. Every order has got those two words tacked on at the end even when she don't say them out loud. *Like Delia*.

One day, this idea pops into my head and I've been nursing it ever since. Maybe I don't want to be like Delia. Maybe I want to be somebody else.

—

All week long I lean toward Sundays, when I slip off to the school with Arthur after Mass. Every single time, Arthur asks whether we got any answer to that letter he wrote, but Miss Lesley shakes her head and tells him to be patient. I can tell he don't like that one bit.

Miss Lesley has a new crazy idea. She says that I should take the certification test for teachers when I'm fourteen so

102

I can go to the Normal School up in Bennington. Arthur is going to be a lawyer according to her, but I could be a teacher. I don't waste breath arguing with her.

She makes us do arithmetic for the first hour and then she turns us to reading and writing. One day she give me a book to take home so I could practice my reading. I slipped it into the house under my smock. I haven't taken it back to her yet 'cause I've only gotten through the first chapter. I don't get much time for reading.

"Grace, you don't walk around anymore when you read," Miss Lesley says to me one day.

I nod without telling her how bad my feet ache. At least in the schoolroom I get to sit for two hours. Henry don't know how lucky he is still to be in school.

The words I'm reading fly around above my head when we start the lesson. But by and by, they drop deep down inside my brain and stay there. Seems I'm hungry for the learning now that it's crammed into those two hours every week.

But I don't like Arthur getting too far out ahead of me. I can still read second best, but my fingers act as stiff and clumsy as ever when it comes to the writing.

⌒

One Sunday Miss Lesley folds her hand over mine to direct the pencil and I cry out. She uncurls my fingers and stares at the big cut in the middle of my palm.

"Albert took a bite of me yesterday," I tell her.

"Who's Albert?" She starts to clean my cut with a rag dipped in something cool, but it stings.

"My worst frame."

"She calls them all names," Arthur explains.

"What are the others?" Miss Lesley asks.

"George, Edwin, Thérèse, Bernadette and Marie," I spit out. She's still poking at my hand with that cloth, making it hurt more.

"You doff six frames?" she says.

"Her mother's the best spinner in the room," says Arthur. It surprises me that he's even noticed with all the time he spends studying the world outside the grimy windows. "So she's got the most machines."

"That makes it hard on Grace," says Miss Lesley. They're talking over my head again as if I'm just one of the floorboards.

"I can do it," I say, and at last she lets go of my hand.

"You've got to keep that cut clean, Grace, or it will get infected."

"Miss Lesley, how much is twelve times one hundred and thirty-six?"

"You figure it. You know how."

It takes me a while what with the carrying over and getting all the numbers in the right columns.

"What's your answer, Grace?"

"One thousand six hundred and thirty-two." She leans over me to check.

"That's right."

"That's how many bobbins she doffs," Arthur says without looking up from his book. Seems he can read and do arithmetic and stick his nosy self into everybody's business all at the same time.

104

"It's a wonder you don't have more cuts," Miss Lesley says.

It's a wonder my hands don't fall off.

⌣

One day Papa stands behind me at the store and makes me read out loud to him every item Mr. Dupree puts on the list. Everybody knows that Mr. Dupree charges things to the mill workers' bills that he takes home himself. I'm the only one in the family who can read and count well enough to catch him at it.

"Grace is a good reader, is she not?" says my father.

Mr. Dupree grunts. He knows exactly what we are about.

"She can write too. Go ahead, Grace. Copy that list for me."

It takes me a long time with that cut-up stubborn right hand. The people behind us in line begin to grumble and stir.

"Now add up the numbers," says my papa.

"Get along now, Joseph," says Norma's mother from her place in the back. "We've all got business here."

"We'll be done soon," Papa says in a loud voice to the whole line. "Grace is quick with numbers."

I show him the total and he reads it to Mr. Dupree. "Now put the date on the top of the page," Papa says to me. "We'll take that home with us. For the record."

Dougie's father standing behind us chuckles. "Looks like you've met your match, Mr. Dupree," he says as we walk on past.

The rest of them make way for us and I like how they look at me. That paper record stays tucked safe in the pocket of my smock. When we get home, Papa puts it away in a jar at the top of the kitchen cupboard.

The next night after supper I'm hauling the wet laundry back up to hang in the kitchen when I stop short at the door. I hear my father and mother talking about me.

"That teacher will put fancy ideas in her head," says Mamère. "The way she's done with Arthur. Boy spends all his time staring out the window, dreaming. Grace is too slow as it is. Even after all this time, I can't count on her the way I could with Delia."

I want to scream no, don't say that, Mamère. Don't say you can't count on me or I'll die the way Claire did. I suck in my breath to stop myself from bursting into the room.

"She's only schooling two hours a week, Adeline. And her learning is doing us some good. Dupree will think twice before he cheats us again."

"Long as she understands that the mill is all she's ever going to have. She needs to settle down and accept that."

There is this silence. Then Papa's voice says, "She's more like you than you know, Adeline."

"How?"

"You didn't settle down and accept the farm. You wanted a better life. She could too."

106

I hear Mamère go into the bedroom and shut the door behind her. Even though the laundry is heavy and wet against my hip, I wait awhile longer before I go inside.

With Pépé gone, it seems there's more room for Papa's voice in the house than there ever was before.

16

THE STRANGER

Arthur is the first one to see the man.

"Mr. Wilson got on the train and same time, someone else got off," he calls in my ear when we pass each other in the row that runs between two of our frames. "A man with a load of boxes. He's coming in the mill."

Ever since we wrote that letter to the Child Labor place, Arthur is waiting for an inspector to come and shut down the mill. I told him over and over that nobody cares about a bunch of us kids in a little nowhere Vermont town, but he says I'm wrong. Whenever the train whistle blows, Arthur manages to get himself over to the window. He needs to keep occupied when those two frames of his mother's are up and running and he's cleared his boards and has nothing to do. Wish I had a minute with nothing to do. If Mamère hadn't tangled with Madame Trottier so many times, we could get Arthur to help me doff. But the two mothers practically spit at each other now every time they get close.

Then the man from the train walks onto the floor. That is strange. Nobody rings a bell or scoots us into the elevator so it means he ain't an inspector. The man is wearing a brown slouch hat, a tie and round glasses pushed up to the top of his long skinny nose. He looks small standing next to French Johnny, but he has big ears. When he takes off his hat, you can see those ears sticking out so far from his head you expect them to wave at you.

⌣

I want to keep watching him, but I make myself stare at my hands 'cause for once they are moving along lickety-split. Ever since I figured out that number with Miss Lesley, one thousand six hundred and thirty-two, I decided I will count each bobbin as I drop it in the box. That keeps my mind tied down to what I'm doing and I figure it makes me practice my numbers at the same time. One morning I counted six sides one after another and told Arthur I'd doffed eight hundred and twelve bobbins so far that day. Arthur said I was wrong 'cause one hundred and thirty-six don't go into eight hundred and twelve. Sometimes I'd like to smack his smart self.

Besides that, Mamère is in a bad mood. George has been giving us trouble all morning and I sure don't want to take any chance with Marie when she is being her so-good self.

When things are singing along like that, it don't matter how many strangers are staring at me from the end of the row.

Before I know it, French Johnny is standing by my elbow breathing his hot-air breath on the place at the top of my head where my braids cross over each other.

"One hundred and thirty-five, thirty-six. Done," I sing out to my mother and her foot lifts to jog the rail.

French Johnny gives her a wave. She lowers her foot to the floor without starting up the frame and goes back over to clear her scavenger rolls.

"This fellow come from the head office to photograph the frames," he says. "You move aside, Grace."

"No," says the man. He has to shake French Johnny's arm and shout to make himself heard. "I want the girl in the picture too. For scale."

Neither one of us knows what that word means and he can tell. "It shows how large the machine is if she stands in front," the man explains. "Those are my instructions."

French Johnny cocks his head. One of Delia's frames has gone down.

"Hurry it up," he calls back over his shoulder as he leaves us looking at each other.

17

THE FLASH

The man starts to unpack his equipment. He must be stronger than he looks to be lugging all this stuff on and off trains and up three flights of stairs to the spinning room. He slides a leather pouch off his shoulder and lowers it to the ground ever so slowly as if it's got some kind of treasure inside. Then he unpacks a wooden box with a tube that points straight out of the middle. I can read the name on it and it has the same first letters as mine. Graflex, it says. He props Mr. Graflex up on top of a spindly-looking set of legs splayed out in three directions like a dog trying to stop itself on a hill. Then he comes over to me.

"My name is Lewis Hine," he says, and sticks out his hand. The ends of his fingers are stained all brown-yellow the way my Pépé's were from his cigarettes. I drop into a curtsy. The mill is a strange place to be curtsying, but I've got two new cuts on the top of my right hand and one on the inside and I don't need to stir them up.

His hat tilted to the side, he leans over close, but I pull away quick. He's a strange one. It turns out he is just asking my name. Imagine that. A grown man wanting to know my name.

"Grace," I say, my voice pitched proper so he can hear it through the buzzing in the room.

"How old are you?"

This is a trick question and I know the answer just fine. "Fourteen," I say without a blink.

"Really? You don't look that old. You must be about forty-eight inches tall."

"How do you know?" He talks to me easy the way Arthur does so it don't feel strange to be asking him questions. I can see Arthur out of the corner of my eye watching us the whole time and I like that, for once, Arthur don't know what's going on and I do.

"I measure you against my vest buttons. You come up to number three. That makes you four feet tall."

Now why would this man care how tall I am? Maybe the head office wants to know the size of the workers. I hope that's not some new way of figuring out how old we are.

"What are you going to do to me?" I ask.

"Take your picture, that's all. Have you ever had your picture taken?"

"Will it hurt?"

"No, Grace. There will be a flash for a second, which will make your eyes sparkle because the room will be a thousand times brighter than it's ever been before. Don't blink if you can help it. Now I need you to stand here," he says, and sets me up in front of Marie.

I lean against her and rest my arm on her thread board. When I look up, a handle's popped up out of the top of Mr. Graflex and Mr. Hine is peering down inside like he's looking for something. The tube sticking out has a big old eye at the end of it and that's sliding out toward me and then moving away again. I stick out my tongue at it and when he looks up again, he's chuckling to himself. So he must have seen me, even though he was staring down into Mr. Graflex's innards. He goes around to the front of the camera and flips a little lever no bigger than a lapette right on the edge of the eye.

I walk over to watch.

"Grace, I meant you to stay by the frame," he says. "Now I'll have to focus again."

I reach out and touch the black folds that push the eye back and forth. "My father's accordion looks like this."

"Those are the bellows," he says. "Now, when you go back to your machine, don't stand too close. I don't want you to hurt yourself."

I laugh. "Marie won't hurt me," I tell him. "She's my good girl."

He looks confused.

"My frame. You've got Monsieur Graflex and I've got Mademoiselle Marie."

"You don't miss much, do you, Mademoiselle Grace," he says, and he's smiling again.

"No, I don't," I say. I wish my mother would tell me something like that. "What's in your pocket?"

He glances around nervously.

"Don't worry. French Johnny ain't paying no attention," I tell him. "He's working on Delia's clearing boards. She's my sister and she's got two of the worst frames in the room. What's in your pocket?" I ask again.

He slides out the most perfect little notebook I've ever seen and a pencil. "I'm taking notes."

"About me?"

"Yes. Your name and height and the age you say you are."

"You take notes in your pocket?"

"It's a trick I learned a long time ago. I keep the pencil pressed against the paper and the paper pressed against my leg bone. Most times I can read what I've written. Can you read?"

"Sure. I can count and spell too. Give me the little book and I'll show you." He pulls it out and hands it to me. I squat down to write my name with his nubbly pencil, but just like he said, it's there already. Miss Lesley would tell him his writing is nothing but a messy scribble, but I can make it out. *Grace, 48 inches, says she's 14.* He's been doing these notes the whole time we've been talking with his hand hidden in his pocket.

"How many sides do you doff?" he asks. He's pulling a black square thing out of his shoulder pouch.

"Twelve."

"That's a lot."

"My mother is top spinner and she's got six frames. Six times two makes twelve sides. One hundred and thirty-six bobbins to a side times twelve makes one thousand six hundred and thirty-two."

He looks surprised by how high I can count. "How many of you kids work in the mill?"

"About twenty or so."

"Put down their names and ages for me," he says. He's already figured out how to make his voice cross under the noise in the room.

Now he's opening the back of the camera, sliding in the metal square from his pouch, and I can tell his hands know what they're doing. He's as fast with his picture-taking machine as Mamère is with her frames.

Arthur, I write. *12. Dougie. 10.* He just started last week. Henry told us it put Miss Lesley in one of her bad moods when French Johnny come for him. *Briget. 13.* Her name looks funny but I keep going. The little pencil keeps digging into the cut on the inside of my hand, but I pay no mind. My letters are slanting the way Miss Lesley likes, but each one takes such a long time. If Arthur was the one doing the writing, he'd be finished by now.

"You go to school?" Mr. Hine asks.

"Not no more. But Miss Lesley gives me and Arthur lessons on Sundays." Now I'm the one checking to see who's listening to us. "I won't tell about your pocket notes if you don't tell about my schooling."

"Deal," he says. "I'd like to meet this Miss Lesley." Now he's shaking some white powder like flour onto a flat box on the floor.

"The school's up the hill," I tell him. I tuck the notebook deep into the folds of my skirt 'cause I can feel Mamère poking her head around every time she gets to the end of a row. Edwin is down ready to be doffed and Thérèse

115

is going to be right behind. Looks like I'll be working through the break. But I don't care right now. I love the little notebook so much I want to steal it.

"Grace, do you know a boardinghouse in town where I can spend the night?"

"We take boarders," I say, and my mind is racing ahead. This man with his tie and his suit, he looks richer than the other ones who stayed in Pépé's bed. "But it's one dollar," I shout louder than I mean to. He don't seem to blink at the price, but the light is reflecting off his glasses so I can't really see his eyes. "And you have to pay before you eat."

"That'll be fine. Where do you live?"

"Up on French Hill. The Forcier place. Everybody in town knows where it is." I want to turn somersaults. Won't Mamère be pleased when she finds out. A whole dollar coming into the house 'cause of me.

"Time to give it back," he says with his hand out. He means the notebook.

"I haven't written all the names yet."

"I can get the rest of them later." He's talking fast now, his voice close to my ear. "Grace, I want to take a picture of all the kids in the mill. Can you get them to meet me after work?"

"Where?" He talks to me as if we are both workers and we have a job to do. Together.

"Outside the mill gates. Can you do that?"

"Sure," I say with a shrug, but I'm not sure. We all scatter like bugs when the mill bell rings. I'll make Arthur help me.

French Johnny is starting down the row toward us.

"Give the notebook back now."

"I wish I had one of these," I say, but I hand him the little book and it disappears quick into his pocket. He sets me back up in the same place, leaning against Marie.

French Johnny and Mamère almost crash into each other at the end of the row and now they're both headed our way.

"Three of my frames are waiting on Grace," Mamère says loudly. "You're taking too much time, mister."

Mr. Hine ain't looking at me. He's staring back down into the hood at the top of the camera and making that eye scoot forward and back again. Finally it stops. We stare at each other. I can see a little tiny me in the eye at the end of the tube and for a second, this scared feeling fills up my throat.

"Stand away, all of you," he says to the others, and his chin is tucked so far down that his voice sounds like it's coming from under a rock.

Mamère and French Johnny pull off to the side as if the three-legged dog with its funny box head might bite them. I'm glad I'm resting against Marie. She makes me feel safe.

"Hold very still, Grace." Mr. Hine pulls a black square thing straight up from the back of the camera just as he calls to me in a sharp voice, "Keep your eyes open as long as you can."

"Don't you hurt her—" I hear my mother say, and the eye of the camera opens wide suddenly as if it means to gobble me up. Then everything happens at once. With one hand he throws a match onto the powder while he squeezes a black bulb at the end of a cord with the other. There's a

117

flash and everything goes white like something has blown up right in the middle of my eyeballs. Smoke tickles my nose. Inside my closed eyes, I can see circles floating out wider and wider from a middle black dot. That's the way an echo would look if you could draw it, I think.

"What the devil was that?" roars French Johnny.

"Grace, open your eyes," my mother shouts in my ear, shaking me all the while. "She's blind, she can't see."

"She's fine," says Mr. Hine, his voice near now, and I feel his hand come to rest on the top of my head. "Don't worry, Mrs. Forcier."

I like them all squabbling over me for that moment, but I know I can't wait no longer so I open my eyes. First I see something that looks like the ghost of Mr. Hine hunched over his camera just at the moment when he squeezed that bulb and the light flashed. But he's not there no more. He's right beside me talking over my head to French Johnny. The ghost picture fades and next, I make out Arthur, who's standing by his frame for real. He's mouthing some words at me over and over again, and pointing at Mr. Hine's back.

"He's the one," Arthur's saying.

And suddenly I know what he means.

Mr. Hine is the answer to our letter.

18

THE GROUP PICTURE

Mamère cuffs me on the head when she finds I didn't go blind. I barely feel it, but there is no reason to hit me. I was just doing what French Johnny and Mr. Hine told me to do.

When Mr. Hine says he only has a couple more pictures to take, French Johnny tells him to pack up his equipment and move on out. It was the flash and the smoke that scared French Johnny the most. Fire can gobble up a mill in no time 'cause there's so much to burn. All that cotton dust in the air and the threads whirling around just waiting for some little spark to light on them.

And suddenly, like things clicking into place in the back of my brain, I remember Mr. Wilson getting on the train that morning. So French Johnny was in charge and he's the one who let in Mr. Hine. And if the mill had burned down when Mr. Wilson was away then fat French Johnny was going to be in a big barrel of trouble.

"That man is *fou, complètement fou,*" mutters Mamère.

I stop in my tracks to tell her the good news.

"Mr. Hine is boarding with us tonight. He knows he's got to pay before he eats."

"Well, that'll make up some of the money he stole from our paycheck fooling with you," she says.

Here is the big surprise. "It'll make up more than you think, Mamère," I say. "I told him he had to pay a dollar and he said fine. He'd be there."

She stares at me with a little look that says, Well, Grace, sometimes maybe I *can* count on you. She don't say it out loud, but her face says it. At least that's what I decide to think.

When Arthur passes me in the row, he says, "I was right, wasn't I? He's the one."

"He wants to get all the kids together after work. To take a picture. You tell them?"

"Where?"

I have to think fast. "Around the front side between the big door and the little hill." The mill owners are the only ones who ever use that front door.

Arthur nods and moves away quick when his mother waves to him.

It ain't till later when I am catching up with my doffing that I think of something terrible. If Arthur is right about Mr. Hine being the answer to the letter, then that committee might shut down the mill and we won't have jobs no more. And this Mr. Hine is spending the night in our house, in Pépé's bed. What if he tells Mamère what he's trying to do?

He won't tell Mamère. He'll just make secret notes in his little book.

120

Yes, he will. He'll tell her and she'll order him out of the house.

So what? Long as we got his dollar who cares about Mr. Hine?

But I like him. I want to talk to him more. I want to see if he'll give me a notebook to write in. And what if he tells Mamère about the letter?

Who cares about the letter? It was signed with that long word. Miss Lesley said nobody would ever guess who wrote it.

Mamère will know. She knows Miss Lesley wants to keep us kids out of the mill. And she hates her. If she gets Miss Lesley fired, then I can't go to school no more.

All this thinking is what my bad brain does. It makes me forget where I am, so sure enough Edwin's clearing board fills up and ten ends in a row go down. I yell to Mamère, who throws the shipper handle with such a look and shoves me aside the way she does when she wants to piece up fast as possible.

Mr. Hine's dollar is getting used up before it even hits our kitchen table. After that, I shut my brain down. I don't let myself think about anything but counting bobbins. Even so there is no way to make up all the time lost on Mamère's hank clock and there is nobody to blame for that but me.

When the closing bell goes, I scoot over to Arthur and we race down the stairs before anybody can stop us.

⌣

Mr. Hine is waiting around the corner of the mill when Arthur and I lead the pack of kids past the gate and down a little path.

"Where are you all going?" the guard yells after us.

"To play a game," I yell back, and he don't pay us no mind after that.

"Grace," Mr. Lewis Hine says first thing. "I need you to help me." Just like we are old friends and I've been helping him for years. The others stare at me in surprise. This man needs Grace, the bumbling left-handed doffer, who's always in trouble? they're thinking.

"Yes, Mr. Hine," I say smartly.

"Is everybody here?"

I look around and count. Seventeen. "Just about. As many as Arthur and I can get." Delia's not here, but that's fine with me. She'll be helping take Mamère's mind off me.

"I'll do the boys first. It settles them down," he says in a low voice as he unpacks Mr. Graflex from his carrying box. He has a hurrying nature to him and I know why. If he gets caught with that camera again anywhere near the mill, he'll probably get arrested. "Arrange them against the brick wall between that door and the window, shortest in the front. I'll want their names and ages before they leave."

The only reason the boys pay me any mind is 'cause they aren't sure about this man and they are specially careful around the camera. But they do keep horsing around and falling over one another and shifting places. Their hats are all skewed funny. Hubert and Pierre Gagnon lounge about with their arms around each other's shoulders and their chins stuck out, pretending this picture-taking happens every day. Felix stands in front with his arms crossed and his legs spread, looking like *he* owns the mill. Arthur sets himself up in back, acting as if he's the only person in the world, just the way he does when he's got a book in his hand. He stands straight up at attention and waits with a frown on his face like a soldier boy about to be shot.

When Mr. Hine comes up behind me, he uses his voice to still them. Maybe he was a teacher before he started the picture-taking business 'cause a bunch of kids don't seem to bother him one bit.

"I'm going to count backwards from three," he explains to the boys. "Once I've focused the lens, you all must stay absolutely still. You'll see me pull a black shade out of the side of the camera. That's the dark slide. At that moment, the negative is ready to be exposed. Once I squeeze the little black bulb with my right hand, you'll see me push that shade back in again. Then you can relax."

They nod, serious now, as if they understand one word he's saying.

"Are you all ready?"

They take up their positions. He rearranges Julien to stand in back of Dougie and this time they stay put.

"It's not going to hurt them, is it?" Bridget asks me, her hands up shielding her eyes.

"Nah," I say like I know all about it. "He's not even using the flash this time the way he did with me."

Just as he said, he pulls the slide out and slams it back in so quick that nobody knows he's all done and they stay frozen.

"Done, boys," he says with his notebook out now.

123

"Starting in the back row." He points at Arthur. "I want your name, your age, your job and how long you've worked in the mill."

"Is this for the head office?" Hubert asks.

Mr. Hine don't answer the question 'cause he's too busy scribbling down *Arthur Trottier, age 12, doffer, 3 months*.

19

UP THE HILL

Next picture he herds us all together, boys and girls. He stands me in the front. I can't really see the eye of Mr. Graflex when it opens and closes 'cause the sun is so low in the sky it's making me squint.

"We can't stay no longer," I tell him. "Chores to do."

Not to mention that my feet are hurting bad and Mamère is going to chop my head off. He nods, still scribbling, and everybody bolts, some up the hill to Mr. Dupree's and beyond to their houses. When he looks up from the notebook, it's just him and me and Arthur.

We help him pack up. I take the spindly dog legs that don't weigh much. Arthur staggers around when he first tries to lift the leather pouch. It's holding all those black squares Mr. Hine slides in and out at the back of the camera.

"I can't afford to have you drop those glass plates," he warns Arthur. "That's two days of work right there."

"I've got them," says Arthur. I can see the strap digging into his shoulder, but he don't complain. Mr. Hine walks right close behind him on our way up the hill just in case Arthur should slip.

"Are you the reader Miss Lesley told me about?"

"We both are," Arthur says, and that surprises me.

"He's the best, I'm second best," I say. "But he can write better than me."

"You did just fine this morning in my notebook."

"I'm slow."

"Her right hand don't work as good as her left," Arthur explains. I don't need him telling people my business, but for once, I let him be.

"When did you see Miss Lesley?" I ask.

"I went by the school. She thinks you kids shouldn't be in the mill."

"She's right," says Arthur.

"You have to keep quiet about all that at our house," I warn Mr. Hine. "Or you can't board over. You promise?"

"I promise. Your parents want you working, then."

"Of course. We need to eat and pay the rent and the store bill," I say. I mean to sound like Mamère and I do.

"You did come 'cause of the letter, didn't you?" Arthur asks.

"Did you write it?"

He looks shifty. "I wrote the words down."

"And I expect Miss Lesley told you what to say."

"We both helped her," I tell him.

Arthur's leaning into the hill with that heavy pouch slung across his back. "I'm getting out of the mill fast as I can," he pants.

126

"How are you going to do that?"

"I've got plans."

"We've got some of our own too, young man. You wait for us to take care of it."

"Your committee?" I ask.

"That's right."

"Grace says you won't bother with a bunch of mill kids in this little town," Arthur tells him.

"I came here, didn't I?"

"You can't shut the mill down," I cry. "Where would we go without jobs?"

"We're not shutting down the mills. My pictures are going to show people out there what your lives are like. Then you won't have to work such long hours and you'll get to stay in school at least till you're fourteen."

I don't bother arguing with him about my age. I've got big feet, but my arms are scrawny. No matter how many birth papers Mamère pulls out of the trunk, I know I don't look fourteen.

"We've already got laws," Arthur says. "Nobody pays them no mind. Besides, you can buy fake papers that say you're old enough."

"Is that what you two did?"

"My mother got some," I say quickly. Everything we tell Mr. Hine is sure to end up in his little notebook. I don't want him to write notes about my dead sister. That's private.

"French Johnny didn't even bother asking for my papers," Arthur tells him. "After my father died, I had to work or we couldn't stay in mill housing. French Johnny says he was doing us a favor." Arthur spits out this last idea like it was giving him a bad taste in his mouth.

Mr. Hine stops in the road and takes out his notebook. "How many of the kids can read?" he asks.

Arthur wiggles the strap over his head and lowers the leather pouch to the ground. He looks glad to be putting it down. "Me and Grace. Her brother Henry's starting."

"Norma can't. Rose can't," I say, going around the old classroom in my head. "Thomas pretends. My older sister Delia can write her name and read a little of the prayer book at Mass."

"Dougie can't. Julien don't even speak English. Neither do Hubert or Lucien. They didn't go to the school at all."

We go on listing the names while Mr. Hine scribbles away. Finally, he says, "I'd like to take a picture of the two of you."

He takes it right then and there, with me and Arthur standing side by side in the grass. Mr. Graflex don't scare me no more. When his eye starts moving toward us, I just glare right back at him, like the two of us are fixing to fight. Arthur stands easy this time, shoulder to shoulder with me, his hands on his hips. I can't see him but I know he's got that "So what do you want?" look on his face.

"You and your committee better hurry up," Arthur tells Mr. Hine when he's saying goodbye. "I'm not waiting much longer."

"I'm doing what I can."

Mr. Hine sticks out his right hand. Arthur stares at it for a moment as if he don't know what it's there for. Then he wipes the grease off his own best as he can and shakes.

20

DINNER

When Mamère sees Mr. Hine standing behind me on the doorstep, she shuts her mouth against what she was going to say.

Henry yanks open the screen door.

"Hello, young man," says Mr. Hine. "Good to see you again."

"Bonsoir, monsieur."

Hine's got that hand of his out again, this time pointed at Papa, who puts his pipe back in his mouth so he can shake it.

"Thank you for letting me board with you tonight," Mr. Hine says. "I understand from Grace that I'm to pay first." He pulls a silver dollar out of a mess of stuff in his pocket and lays it on the kitchen table.

For a minute we all stare at it as if it's a live thing before Papa snatches it up with a nod and tucks it away in his shirt pocket.

"We're not fancy," Mamère says. She points over at Pépé's corner. "That's your bed. We'll eat presently. You can wash your hands outside at the pump."

"I'll show him," I say.

"No," says my mother. "Delia's going down to the basement with the first load of laundry. She can show him on the way. Grace, I need you to do some work for a change."

"Grace was working pretty hard in the mill this morning," Mr. Hine says, and I cringe. Be quiet, I mouth in his direction, but he's already following Delia out the door.

I set his dog legs down in the corner by the bed and pick up the first potato that needs peeling.

"Where have you been?" Mamère asks.

"Showing Mr. Hine the way up here to French Hill."

"You've been gone longer than that. Did you walk him all the way to Massachusetts and back?"

"He needed to take some more pictures."

"Good thing he's scrawny. Maybe he won't eat much."

The screen door opens again and I feel Mamère stiffen beside me. I hope Mr. Hine don't say nothing more to set her off. She can be touchy at the end of a long day like this, especially when our hank clock numbers are way down. She'll take it out on me, but it was as much his fault as mine.

Suddenly he pulls up next to me and starts in peeling a potato. I never seen a man do that before. Except for Pépé.

"No cause for that," Mamère says across the top of my head. We're all three standing in a row. "You'll get your supper."

"My mother and father owned a little restaurant back home. This comes to me naturally."

"Where's back home?" Delia asks from where she's laying the table. Usually she don't talk to strangers the way I do, but he must have made friends with her at the pump. He makes friends quickly.

"Oshkosh, Wisconsin," barks Henry as if it's the answer to a test question.

"Good memory, son."

"How do you know that?" I ask Henry. Suddenly Mr. Hine ain't mine no more. It feels like everybody owns a piece of him.

"Miss Lesley made him give us a talk about his life and then we looked at his camera. And he took a picture of us."

"So you know Miss Lesley?" Mamère asks later when we're settling around the table. I suck in my breath and hold it. Let's not start talking about her.

"No, ma'am. I only just met her this afternoon. She seems a good teacher."

"*Notre Seigneur,*" says Papa. We bow our heads for the blessing and I thank God for the food and pray that Mamère will forget about Miss Lesley for once.

She don't.

"That Mademoiselle Lesley may know how to teach, but she wants to keep our children from working in the mill. It's not for her to decide."

Dear God, I pray again. Please keep Mr. Hine quiet. Then I stare across the table at him with my eyes very big as a warning.

131

He's not looking at me when he opens his mouth to say something, but Papa speaks first.

"What is your job, Mr. Hine? Why are you taking all these pictures?"

This time I try poking my foot across the table to knock him in the knee, but I hit the wrong person.

"Grace, what are you doing?" Delia cries. She pushes my bare foot away, then wipes her hand off on her napkin. More grease on her smock.

"I take pictures of machines. And the people who work with them."

"And the school?" Mamère asks, her voice sharp.

"And the school. The mill owners pay to run it, so they want to be sure Miss Lesley is giving them their money's worth."

I start breathing again. I don't know if he's telling the truth or making up a pile of lies, but I can see Mamère smiling a little. Maybe it's 'cause of what he's saying about Miss Lesley. More likely, it's 'cause Mr. Hine didn't ask for seconds even though his one small helping of stew was mostly potatoes.

And the dollar I got him to pay is already safely stowed away in Papa's shirt pocket.

After dinner, it's my turn at the washing.

"Hang the clothes inside, Grace," my mother says. "It smells like rain to me."

"Could I go down with Grace to the basement?" Mr. Hine says.

Now why would he want to do that?

He answers the question nobody asked out loud. "I need

132

the use of a sink and some water to develop my glass negatives."

We're all still standing there, hands in midair. This man is speaking English, but not words any of us know.

"What does that mean?" I finally ask.

"He makes the camera draw the pictures on pieces of glass," Henry says.

"How can that be?" asks my father.

"Henry's almost right. I actually use a chemical solution to make the pictures show themselves on the surface of the glass."

"No fire?" my mother says.

"No, ma'am. No fire this time."

"Grace has a pile of washing to do," my father says.

"I can help her," Mr. Hine says. "So the sink gets freed up faster."

Imagine a grown man doing the laundry. Mr. Hine is *complètement fou*, my mother is thinking. And she may be right. But I don't care. Anybody who wants to help me with the washing is welcome to join me in the basement.

21

THE GHOST GIRL

He's a good scrubber, but he gets mad when the grease don't come out. I have to move him along or else we'll spend all night in the basement fussing over the hem of Mamère's skirt.

"You a smoker?" I ask.

"No."

"Your fingers are colored dark like my Pépé's. He said it was from the cigarettes he used to smoke."

"It's the developing chemicals," he says.

Now he's scrubbing away at his fingers. They're like the dress. They don't come clean either.

"Does your Pépé live with you?"

"He did but he left," I say. "You're sleeping in his bed."

"Where did he go?"

My throat feels like it's closing up. "Back to Canada. He

don't like me working in the mill either. He wants me to go with him."

"Will you?"

I shake my head. I don't want to talk about Pépé no more. "Are you married?" I ask.

"Yes."

"What's your wife's name?"

"Sara Ann. She's angry with me at the moment."

"Why?"

"Because I'm always on the road taking my pictures. Sometimes she travels with me, but not this time. She wants me home."

"Do you have children?"

"Not yet. But I used to be a teacher."

"I figured that," I say. "The way you act with kids."

"Why?"

"You're not scared of a bunch of us all together and you're not mean to us. Seems you're used to kids."

"Maybe I even like them," he says.

"Miss Lesley wants me to take the test for the Normal School so's I can learn how to be a teacher."

"I trained at a Normal School myself. Miss Lesley is right. You should do it, Grace."

I roll my eyes. "I'm a doffer and one day I'll be a spinner," I say. "That's my life." But even as I'm saying it, I know some little corner of me is hoping it's not true. "Leave it be," I say, snatching Mamère's green skirt away from him. "The grease never comes out completely. Even if it did, it'll just be back tomorrow."

"Let me try one more time."

"No," I say firmly, as I feed it through the wringer. "I'm not going to waste no more time on a smock that's going to spend next week mopping up the mill floor."

What I don't say is that my feet are swollen so big from standing that it feels as if the blood might burst through the skin. And I have to stand on them all day tomorrow and the next day and the one after that. But I'm not ready to leave. I want to see what he does with those pieces of glass he's been hauling around.

So finally when the clothes are hanging on the line above our heads, we carry in three full buckets of water from the pump. Then he shuts the door against the last bit of light and turns up the kerosene lantern he's hung from the clothing line. It glows red. His face takes on the color and mine must too.

"What's that for?"

"That's called a safelight. It lets us see what we're doing, but it keeps the picture safe so it doesn't develop too quickly. You remember the way I store my negatives in their holders? That's so the light doesn't hit them. Bright light will make the images come too fast."

It sounds as if he's delivering babies.

"Rose's baby brother come too early and he died. The pictures can die too?"

Mr. Hine's face looks gloomy. "Pictures die for lots of reasons," he says. "If the subject doesn't stand absolutely still, then the image comes out blurry. Or if the flash powder doesn't light, then the picture's too dark and you can't see anything. Or if I drop the glass plate, then there's no picture at all."

No wonder he stuck so close when Arthur was walking up that hill carrying his precious pouch.

He sets up four tin trays in a row. He leaves the first one empty, pours half a bucket of water into the middle one and powder from a little bottle into the third one. He makes me put water in there too.

"Shake it back and forth a little," he tells me. "Good. Now we're just about ready."

"How does it work?"

"First one is the developer, second the rinse, third the fixer. That stops the developing right where you want it. And the last one is another rinse."

One by one, he pulls the glass plates in their wooden holders from the pouch and leans them up against the wall. They look like a line of kids waiting to be picked for a prize.

"How do you know which one's me?"

"The notebook," he says, sliding it out of his pocket and leafing through the pages. "I keep a record of each picture as I take it. Here you are. Number fourteen."

I lift it so's to carry it over to where the trays are lined up.

"Careful," he says. I am watching every step I take. Even though it don't make no sense to me, he says this piece of glass has got me trapped inside it. I certainly don't intend to drop myself.

With my hands tight on the wooden frame, he pulls out that dark metal piece the way he did just before he squeezed the bulb that set off the flash and started all the commotion. Then he flips down the edge of the holder so he can slide the piece of glass free.

"The surface is coated when I buy it," he says as he lowers "me" carefully into the first empty tray. "You must be careful never to touch it because finger marks will show up in the final print." He pours a little bit of liquid from a vial onto the sheet of glass and then rolls that puddle back and forth until it drips off all the edges.

"Watch," he says, whispering now. Suddenly, like magic, the glass is changing. Dark spots come up a little bit at a time and then faster. It's hard to see what they are because the tray underneath is black and the red lantern makes so little light in the room.

"All the dark places you see here will be white in the final picture. That's why it's called a negative. The final paper print, the positive, is the photograph," he tells me, his voice as low as a prayer. It's as if he don't dare talk too loud or the magic spots will disappear on him. But I don't see why he's so worried. Those spots don't look like me or anybody else that I can make out.

I put my nose closer. The nasty smell makes me pull away as he lifts the plate from that tray and slides it into the rinse. If I am there, I'm drowning under all the water he's swishing back and forth.

"Follow me," he says, walking to the corner. He holds up the glass piece right in front of the white sheet we just washed. The water drips off onto my bare feet. "There you are."

I can't make my brain understand what I am seeing. A black-skinned girl with white hair is staring out at me from her deep dark eyeholes. It looks like that developing of his conjured up a ghost.

We're both silent, studying on the person trapped in the glass, who's looking right at me. She is holding still the way he told me to do, leaning back against a frame.

"I know it's hard to tell from the negative," he says, his voice quiet. "I'll send you a copy of the print once I get home. Look closely now. That's your smock with the fat pockets and your arm leaning up against your machine. What do you call her?"

"Marie. But what's wrong with my face?"

"Nothing. You're very pretty. That's the same face you see in the mirror every morning."

"We don't got a mirror."

Delia's always trying to catch sight of her reflection in the store window when we go past on the way to the mill. Whatever for, I wonder.

"Everything you're seeing is in reverse," he says. "So your legs are white and in this picture they're black."

I finally begin to get it. "And my feet are black from the grease, so that's why they're white in the glass here."

"Exactly."

I reach out my finger.

"Don't touch," he warns.

He's right, it is me. You know how I can tell? Marie's got two spindles that are missing their guides. And there they are just below where I'm resting my elbow. Nobody else doffs Marie. So it has to be me. And now I'm looking closer I can make out Delia's old shirt with the little white flowers that got passed down to me and the little checks in my gingham smock. I'm teaching my brain to take everything it's seeing black and turn it around.

139

But there's such a scared look in this ghost girl's face. How could she be me?

I slap him on the arm and he flinches.

"That's not me," I say. "Your notebook is wrong. That's some worried little woman."

"That's you, Grace," he says, and lets out his breath as if he's been holding it.

We stare some more.

"I've got big eyes," I say at last.

"You see that cut?" He glances at my right hand and then back at the picture.

Sure enough, old Mr. Graflex caught it too.

"See what I mean about the grease?" I tell him. "You can't never get it out."

"You don't have shoes?"

"No use messing them up in the mill." I keep wanting to touch my glass self, but he won't let me. "My arms look awful skinny. But they're strong. I can even lift the roving creels for my mother."

"I'm sure you can. You've got to be strong, Grace, to survive in the mill."

He looks at me with such a sad face that I feel like shaking him. Without another word, he takes the negative back over to the third tray, and I trail behind as if he's carrying a piece of me and I can't let him out of my sight. He lowers me into the water mixed with the fixer and leaves me there. I lean over to stare but I can't see nothing. The smell of that one makes me wrinkle my nose, but I don't pull away.

"I disappeared," I cry. I didn't like that ghost girl, but

that's all there was of me. I jiggle the tray and some water sloshes out. "Mr. Hine, come quick."

He's not paying no mind.

"The picture died already."

He looks up finally from his place by the wall. He's working a second piece of glass out from the other side of the holder. "It's all right, Grace. The background is too dark for us to see anything when the negative is resting in the trays. In a few minutes, I'll take it out of there, rinse it again and set it up in a drying rack. Meanwhile I'll start on this one of you and Arthur."

Mr. Graflex has got me trapped inside two more pieces of glass, I know, but suddenly, I don't care no more. I feel limp. My feet are aching something bad.

Above my head, I hear the pounding of my father's boot on the floor. "Grace, *viens ici!*" he orders.

"It's time for the rosary," I tell Mr. Hine.

"Off you go then," he says. "Open the door quickly and be sure to close it tight behind you."

"It's dark out now," I say.

He don't answer. I can feel him waiting for me to go so he can get on with his work. Mamère holds herself the same way when her foot's itching to jog the rail.

"Goodbye," I say. "Maybe I'll see you in the morning."

"Goodbye, Grace. Thanks for your help."

Moment I shove that door to, I know he'll be pouring the liquid over me again. Me and Arthur.

22

GONE

Mr. Hine must have caught the first train out, the one that goes before the mill bell even rings.

Mamère wakes me. Usually it's Delia.

"The man's gone already," she says. "He left you something."

Everybody is gathered around the table staring at the note as if it might bite them. Except for lucky Henry. No need for him to be up this early.

"What does the writing say?" my father asks.

I read the note to myself first.

> Dear Grace,
>   Thank you for your help. I saw you had your eye on that little notebook of mine so I shall send you one of your own with your photograph. I want you

to write down your life so it doesn't disappear on you too quickly. Do everything you can to get yourself to the Normal School for teacher training.

My best regards to your family and to Arthur. Tell him to be patient and bide his time. And please let Miss Lesley know that I will stay in touch as I promised.

Cordially,
Lew Hine

But I don't read it like that to my family. I skip over the part about Miss Lesley and the normal school and the words I don't know. Truth is I do a lot of skipping and some making up.

"Dear Grace," I read. "Thank you for your help. You are a very smart girl. Say hello to your family and Arthur. Lew Hine."

Mamère stands behind me. "That's a lot of words he wrote down when he don't have that much to say," she says. She touches the word *Lesley* and the word *Lew*. "This one looks like this one."

I fold the paper up real quick and tuck it in my pocket. "You have sharp eyes, Mamère. I could teach you to read."

"You teaching Mamère?" Delia cries with a hoot of laughter.

"Hush, Delia," Mamère says, and I wonder what she is thinking. But then the mill bell starts to ring and we're all caught up in the morning scramble.

I hope Mr. Hine keeps his promise and sends me that notebook. Then I'm going to write my life down like he said I should so it don't get swallowed up and forgotten.

—

I give Arthur the message about biding his time, but every day he gets more restless. He's making a rut in the floor going back and forth to that window as if some other person will hop off the train and rescue us from the doffing.

"I'm going crazy," he whispers at me one Saturday weeks later when we're clearing the lint out of the frames. I give him the cleaning hook my father made him, but he still uses his fingers most times. "Same thing every day."

"Except Sunday," I tell him.

"I can't be waiting all week for that one day."

"Mr. Hine is working on it."

He sneers at me. "I bet that Mr. Hine's forgotten us already, Grace. Every man for himself is what I say."

Arthur don't explain no more than that, but later I see him measuring the space between the sprockets in the gearbox, trying to poke the end of a bobbin in there. Maybe he's fixing to shut down the frame, but I don't know what good that will do. They'll get it up and running soon enough and all he'll have to show for himself is lower pay from his mother's hank clock.

All the kids are out of school now and most of them spend their days in the mill the way I used to do. They come and they go, toting dinner pails, sweeping around our feet and playing the same games I remember. They get in my way and I know now how Delia must have felt all those summer days when the mill was a place for me to play and a place she was never going to leave.

It makes me restless too. I sure don't want Mr. Hine and his glass plates to be the most exciting thing that ever happens to me in my whole entire life.

A girl named Valerie's been left with me for training. When her mother died, her father sent her and her little sister, Ora, down from Canada to live with their cousins, the Vallees. Valerie's a quick thing, eager to do the work, and she don't get underfoot like some of them. But she'll slow down like the rest of us when the dullness gets to her.

—

One rainy Sunday we find the schoolhouse all locked up. Arthur bangs on the door, but I can see through the dirty window that nobody's there.

"Maybe the rain held her up," he says. "She'll be along. It's a three-mile walk."

"How long does it take her?" We never walk farther than the mill or down to the river.

He shrugs. "More than an hour."

First time I ever thought about Miss Lesley and that walk to and from her boardinghouse. More than an hour and the fire to light winter mornings. Summers she comes in to watch the kids that are too small to go into the mill. Sunday's the one day she don't need to make the trip. 'Cept for our lessons.

"Maybe she don't want to teach us no more."

He glares at me. "That's crazy thinking, Grace." But I can tell he's worried himself. Miss Lesley's always been there before. If we don't even have Sundays to wait for, then what'll we do to make our lives go by faster?

When we're settling ourselves against the wall to wait, we both spy a piece of paper sticking out from under the door. Arthur gets to it first. He holds it away from me and does all the reading.

> Dear Arthur and Grace,
>
> I was called away on urgent business. Continue your writing exercises this week, Grace. Arthur, I expect a report on The Red Badge of Courage next week.
>
> Miss Lesley

"What does *urgent* mean?" I ask.

"Don't know. But it must be something important or she wouldn't go off like that."

"You didn't tell me you finished the soldier story."

"You didn't ask."

"Henry the soldier fought in the end?"

"He fought like a regular devil. He didn't sit around and wait to get himself killed, I know that."

Then I tell Arthur the bad thing I heard my mother talking about with Delia.

"They're fixing to move your mother to those three frames on the other side of ours next to Delia. They're giving your two to Bridget's mother 'cause with Dougie doffing for her now, she can handle more."

"The back of the room?"

I nod. "But we can still talk 'cause my Edwin shares a row with one of your new ones." I don't tell him how my mother was grumbling on about being stuck next to Madame Trottier and that dizzy boy of hers.

"How do you know?" Arthur asks.

"I heard talk."

He studies on this for a while. I know what he's thinking. He'll die if they move him away from that window. No train to watch, no mountains, no river. Nothing but bobbin counting to mark the time.

"I won't be doing that," he says real quiet and certain.

"You got to."

He just gets up and walks away without even bothering to argue with me.

Suddenly I feel sick deep inside my gut. Pépé floated away up the river and no Miss Lesley for a whole week 'cause of her urgent business and Arthur talking like that and Mr. Hine come and gone with no pictures like he promised to send.

It feels like everybody's moving on to somewhere else and leaving me behind.

23

ARTHUR

Miss Lesley come back the next week. She snuck off to one of those committee meetings up in a little town north of Bennington. She told us she heard there that Mr. Hine took pictures of kids working in all the mills around Vermont and that he was fixing to write up a report with those pictures and send the committee a copy.

"I shall get one also," she tells us.

"He promised to send me pictures," I say. "And a notebook."

"Mr. Hine makes lots of promises," grunts Arthur. They moved him and his mother to the back of the room the day after I told him they would. He barely speaks to me now when we pass in the row. It's not my fault you got moved, Arthur Trottier, I want to say, but I'm leaving him be. I've got this feeling that he'll explode if I so much as look at him crossways.

"Changing minds takes time, Arthur," says Miss Lesley. "I know how you feel, though. I'm as eager to have you back in school full-time as you are to be here."

"I doubt it," he says, and buries his nose back in his new book. She give me a look that says, What's wrong with him? But I just shake my head 'cause for once, I don't know what to tell her.

I'm itching to move my pencil into my other hand the way I've started doing in Mr. Dupree's store when I write down those lists for Papa. But Miss Lesley's standing behind watching me the whole time. The steamy hot air is making my skin stick to the bumpy wood of the desk and I've got to keep waiting for my clumsy right hand to catch up with my brain. I peel one leg off the seat of the chair and then the other. Outside, I can hear the kids yelling down in the shallow part of the river. None of us knows how to swim, but we all know how to cool off on Sundays.

Suddenly this whole schooling business seems stupid to me and I put down the pencil and stand up before I even know what I'm doing.

"Miss Lesley, I am never going to pass no test for the Normal School. I am never getting out of the mill no matter what you say. Sunday is the only day I've got to cool off in the river and that's where I'm going."

At least that makes Arthur lift his face out of his book. They both stare at me for a second without saying nothing. Last time Miss Lesley threw me out of school. Now here I am again quitting on my own.

"You're right, Grace," she says with a nod. "Go on."

I'm halfway down the hill before I wonder what I was

right about. That I'm never passing no test or I'm never getting out of the mill. Or that Sunday is the only day for the river. Or all of it.

It don't matter what she thinks, I tell myself.

—

One afternoon I am doffing Edwin, who shares a row with Mrs. Trottier's first frame. Arthur don't name his machines the way I do.

I can feel Arthur moving along behind me, but I get done first. When I turn around, I see him crouch down to reset the builder. Nothing strange about that 'cause he always does that for his mother. But then he walks back to the gearbox and begins fooling around in there, which is a thing we're never supposed to do. I think, what's he cleaning in there for, it's still early in the week, and then I hear him yell "READY" at his mother and she's got her head down and without her knowing she's gonna be spinning more than thread, her foot finds the rail to jog. The belt moves, the gears turn and Arthur's hand gets picked up and carried around just like he meant it to. Maybe the screaming is coming from me and maybe it's coming from Arthur, but all I know is he's gone and put his fingers in that place between the sprockets and they're chewing his hand all to bits.

I run to his mother, who's lifted her head 'cause of the disturbance, but still she can't see she's spinning her boy's bones into thread and I butt her from behind. I shove her foot off the rail and yell at her to throw the shipper handle,

150

throw it, jumping to try and get it, but in the end it's Mamère who reaches up over both of us and shuts that frame down. Ends are popping all over the place and I can just see the top of Arthur's head where it's lying on the greasy floor. By the time I slide my way up there, French Johnny is lifting him and there's blood mixed with the oil and when Arthur's face bobs past me, flopping along in French Johnny's arms, his eyes are closed and his face looks pasty gray like bread dough.

"Is he dead?" I ask the air, and someone whispers behind me that the boy's hand has been mangled by the machine and he's passed out from the pain.

Whenever I close my eyes, all I see is his hand disappearing into that mess of gears and the sick come up my throat.

⌣

Arthur lost the middle two fingers on that hand. His good one. The one he writes with. The doctor from the next town come and sewed up whatever pieces of the insides were hanging out, and now Dougie says it's all wrapped up in a fat dirty bandage. Arthur ain't been outside the house since it happened, but Dougie peeked in the window to look at him. Dougie would. He don't understand a thing about privacy.

People are talking.

"He must have been trying to clear lint out of the gears."

"It wasn't cleaning day."

"He's a dizzy one."

"Whatever was the boy thinking?"

I'm the only one who knows Arthur was fixing to do whatever he had to so's he could get out of the mill. I just never did imagine he would commit a crime so horrible against his own self. Even if I had figured out what he was planning to do, I was never giving Arthur no cause to call me tattle again. And maybe this time I should have. Thinking like that makes my head pound something terrible.

My mother says nothing for once. That first night when I can't sleep, she makes me up a hot brew of herbs like she used to do for Pépé. When I throw it all up, she still don't say a word, but calls to Papa. He wipes my face down with a wet cloth and holds me in his lap till my stomach stops turning over. I fall asleep like that.

⌣

Mrs. Trottier's machines were down all the rest of that day and the next. When she dragged herself back in on the third day, Mamère and Delia both covered for her when they could. Mamère even sent me over to doff for her twice that afternoon. She was all in a muddle, Arthur's mother. I had to remind her two times to clear her scavenger rolls and she looked at me with these empty eyes like her mind was far away somewhere.

⌣

Not one of us is working with any heart in it. At break, Mamère don't even try to get the women singing. We sit in a circle and chew our food and swallow as if we are pushing rocks down our throats. All I can see is Arthur's hand disappearing inside that gearbox and when Dougie wonders out loud whether pieces of his fingers ended up in the thread, I slap him so hard, he actually shuts up for once and stays as far away from me as he can.

24

THE WOUND

Arthur and his mother don't come to Mass on Sunday, but we pray for them. Mamère leads the singing as usual, but with no organ backing them up, the choir sounds weak and spindly. There ain't a breath of air in that upstairs room 'cause of the terrible hot spell that's dragged on and on. We are all used to the heat, which builds up something fierce in the mill, but being pressed so close to one another with no frames to separate us can make a person feel real sick from breathing in all that body smell. The old-goat stink of the frames is even better than that. Two of the women faint and have to be carried out. Even Père Alain seems happy when Mass is finished.

⁓

I go over to the schoolhouse out of habit. I don't know what else to do with myself.

When I cup my hands to look through the window, I can see Miss Lesley sitting at her desk. She don't got no reason to be there, 'cause I already give it up and Arthur ain't coming.

She's not writing or reading or nothing. She's just sitting there like the heat has knocked her stupefied.

When I tap on the window, she waves me in.

"I thought you'd given up on school, Grace." She sounds as if she has to drag her voice up from the bottom of her feet.

"I'm just visiting," I say, sliding into my old seat.

"Glad to have you," she says, and I think she means it.

After a long time, I say, "I 'spect Arthur will be back in school regular now."

"Don't count on it."

"He can't doff no more."

"Anymore," she corrects me, but with no spirit to it. "There's always work to be found in the mill, Grace, even if you're missing a few fingers. You know that better than I."

I look away. Maybe Arthur tore off two of his fingers for no reason at all. Maybe he needed to give up his whole hand or his arm to keep himself safe from ever working in the mill again.

"It's his writing hand," I say.

She nods, her eyes big and empty. "What his mother must be feeling," she whispers.

I put my head down on the desk 'cause the room is beginning to spin around on me. Must be the heat. She moves by and for just a second, like a breeze ruffling my hair, her hand comes to rest on my braids.

155

She give me some adding to do. "Just to pass the time," she says as if we're both waiting for something to happen.

I like numbers. They fix my jumpy mind in one place for as long as I'm doing the problem. It's the first peace I've had since the accident.

Outside we hear somebody walking slow up the porch steps. We sit and wait, but it's taking this person an awful long time to make his way to the door. We know who it is before he comes into sight.

Arthur leans against the wall and we stare like we're seeing a ghost.

"Arthur," says Miss Lesley.

She's got one hand over her mouth like she's fixing to be sick. We're trying hard both of us not to look at the place where the bandage is coming unraveled. Neither of us wants to see what's left there.

She goes to help him, but he waves her away and slides into Dougie's old seat. I don't think he can make it all the way over to his regular place. His face is still looking doughy and his other hand is shaking bad.

"Oh, Arthur," Miss Lesley cries suddenly. "I warned you and warned you to pay attention."

"I said I was going to take care of things." His voice sounds cracked and old.

"Don't tell me you did this on purpose," she whispers in a shocked voice. How come she didn't figure that out before? She knows him as well as I do. She heard his talk.

"I wasn't getting out of that mill no other way that I could see."

156

Now she's got her hand back over her mouth and her eyes look scared like she really is seeing a ghost.

"Do it hurt bad?" I ask to break up that stare they're locked into.

"Something awful," he says.

Miss Lesley brings him a glass of water from the bucket in the corner and he drinks that one and the next like his body's been suffering from a drought.

"You should be home in bed," she says. "I'll walk you back."

"Nah. I've been there four days now. I told my mother I can't stand it no more. I'll be coming to school tomorrow."

"If that's what you want, Arthur."

"It's the whole reason I did it."

This should make Miss Lesley happy, him wanting so bad to come back to school, but she still looks miserable. My mother would say it's all her fault on account of the foolish ideas she's been putting in Arthur's mind about getting ahead in life. Him a lawyer or a manager. And me a teacher. She's been jogging us with her crazy notions.

"How you gonna write?" I ask. He don't answer me, just starts to unwrap that miserable string of a bandage.

"Leave it alone, Arthur," she cries. "The doctor should be doing that."

"He ain't coming back. He knows we can't pay the bill. Kept saying he shouldn't of bothered with a little thing like this in the first place." He goes on turning the gray strip round and round and we can't take our eyes off what's coming. "Wound needs air," he says. "I read about that in the soldier book."

It looks bad. The place where Arthur's fingers used to be is sealed off with this bright red stitching that's as jagged and uneven as my mending. His whole hand is swollen up so tight that it seems whatever's been stuffed back inside might ooze out through the scar.

"It don't look so good," Arthur says in this low sad voice. What a thing to find that two of your fingers is gone for good, not just folded over and hiding out of sight.

"Arthur," I tell him. "Writing with your other hand ain't so hard as you think. You get used to it. I'll show you."

I don't know if he hears me. He's sagging down in the chair like the fight's leaked out of him all at once.

⌣

Miss Lesley and I walk him home, one on each side, holding him up between us. The people we pass stop and stare and shake their heads but they don't get near. Bad luck like Arthur's could be catching.

His mother is waiting at the door like she's been expecting us. The two of them get Arthur into bed. He falls asleep before he's even lying down.

"Miss Lesley, I want to speak to you, please." Something in Mrs. Trottier's voice sounds strong and sure like she's made up her mind in one direction. If I didn't know, I'd think it was Mamère talking.

"I'm so sorry. How terrible this must be for you—" Miss Lesley starts to say, but Mrs. Trottier waves her hands at the other woman the way you slap at a bug that's annoying your face. "Excuse me, but pity don't help me none right now. I need something else from you. Mr. Trottier has a cousin in New Hampshire and I want to ask the man for money. Can you write the letter? Today?"

Miss Lesley sinks into a chair and for once, she looks like the student who's been given handwriting practice. "Of course. I'll do it now."

It turns out that the Trottiers don't have no paper, so Miss Lesley sends me back to the schoolhouse and by the time I go down the hill and up again, I am sweaty and tired myself.

When I come in, Arthur is flipping back and forth and groaning something terrible. His mother gives me a wet cloth that ain't too clean and tells me to wipe his face and his arms.

"It will bring the fever down," she says, but she don't even let Arthur's torment distract her from that letter.

Except for family, I don't usually get that close to a body, specially Arthur. For once he's not giving me his regular look that says, What d'you want from me? He's got this nice little spread of freckles that travel over his nose from one cheek to the other. His upper lip has a wrinkle in it that's deeper than the one in mine. His ears stick out some and they're big. They make me think of Mr. Hine and that first time I saw him looking at me from down the row. He never did send us no pictures and he don't know that Arthur is lying here missing two fingers with this sweet sickly smell coming up off his wound. And suddenly I feel lower than a snake's belly, as my Pépé used to say, and I start to cry about all the things that have not gone right for me and Arthur. I don't make one sound and the two women are hunched over the table, so they take no notice.

Crying wears a body out. It's one reason I don't ever let it happen, but this time it took me by surprise. I'm fixing to lie down and rest right next to Arthur on his skinny excuse for a bed when Miss Lesley says, "Grace. I hear someone calling you."

Sure enough it's Delia. Means Mamère is angry. She's been putting up with my Sunday schooling without saying nothing, but I better be home right after.

I fold the wet cloth and press it down on Arthur's forehead to make it stick in place. He's calmed down some.

"See you," I say.

His eyes fly open at that and he stares up at me like I'm a stranger he's never seen before.

That's the worst. I run from that house without saying goodbye.

25

TEACHER

Mamère is trying to learn herself reading. I catch her at it, running her fingers over the letters on the stove.

"That's an *A*," I say, and she snatches her hand back like it was burned. "*Adeline* starts with *A*." The whole thing says ACME CHARM NEWARK STOVE WORKS, CHICAGO, but I don't confuse her with all that. I don't know what it means myself.

I pick her finger back up and run it over the *E* in *Acme*. "The *E* is in all our names. *Delia, Grace, Henry, Adeline, Joseph*. Even *Pépé*."

She points to the C. "What's this one?"

"That's a C. For *creel, carding, combing*." I'm thinking fast as I can. "*Claire*."

She gives me her steady look.

"It comes right before *D*. For *Delia, doffing*. And right after *B* for *bobbins, boy, belt*."

"What's this last letter?"

"M. For *Mamère*."

—

It gets to be a game between us. Suddenly she's finding letters all over the place where she's never seen them before. The frames got names on them down near the gearboxes. They say Fales and Jenks and I tell her the letter J is the same one that starts the word Joseph, which is Papa's name.

When I bring home supplies from the store, she picks out the different letters on the sacks and packages and I read her the words. *Flour. Sugar. Matches.* Pretty soon I see her lips moving all the time, but she ain't praying. She's saying the alphabet.

When I tell Miss Lesley that I'm teaching my mother to read, she gives me books to take home to her. They're the baby books that Henry and me started with, but Mamère don't seem to care. She studies over them under the kerosene lamp like she's figuring out some map to somewhere new. Everybody tiptoes around her and nobody in the family says one word against it. Papa even plays the accordion those nights out on the front stoop 'cause the music calms her and helps her to think.

One night through the wall, I hear him say, "Adeline, you are something."

"What?"

"Always fixing your eye on the next place to get to."

She don't answer, least not loud enough for me to hear.

162

One Sunday when I'm hanging around after Mass, Mamère gives me a pinch.

"What're you doing?" she asks me. "It's time for your schooling."

"I give it up. I don't go no more."

She studies me. "You know as much as Miss Lesley then?"

"No."

"Then go. You can quit when I tell you it's time."

My mother is a confusion to me, but I trot off down the hill without arguing. Truth is I've been missing the Sundays now that the weather has cooled off. Besides, I may get to see Arthur.

Without him, the mill is real lonely. When we were both doffing, I didn't get to talk to him much, but I could feel him moving up and down his frames when I was working mine. Valerie's gone over to doff for Mrs. Trottier, but it ain't the same. We don't have no history together.

Mrs. Trottier is different now. Mamère says the accident, which is what we all call it, sharpened her up and I guess she's right. Even French Johnny says she's up to speed. That's what the hank clock shows and the hank clock don't ever lie. I hear her snapping at Valerie and hurrying her along. I expect it's so she can get home to Arthur.

Maybe she's thinking that if she keeps up her numbers, nobody will bother her about Arthur being back in school. Miss Lesley talks all over town about what a help Arthur is with the little kids, but she's not fooling me. I know Arthur just sits in the back and reads to himself like he's always done. He's the only big kid left in there. Even Thomas got a job with a farmer upstate who don't care about his twisted foot, long as he can get about the place and work the horses. Papa says farming work ain't so precise as mill work. You can do it at your own pace with no hank clock counting.

Arthur's hand is still healing. It don't look so raw, but nobody sees it much 'cause he keeps it hidden up inside his shirtsleeve most of the time.

So I go down the hill to school like Mamère told me to, but when I get there the room is empty. Of course. Miss Lesley don't think I'm coming back. And Arthur don't need to go to school on Sundays. He's there now all the other days. Getting ahead of me.

The latch lifts easy. For some reason, she didn't lock up. I go into the empty room.

It ain't so bad being in the place by myself. I settle down at my desk and since nobody's there to watch, I practice writing with my left hand. I love the way my pencil scoots across the page and fills it up fast. I'm copying over a page from my fifth reader. It's a poem called "Nathan Hale" and I know Arthur would like it 'cause it has soldiers and drums and flags in it.

When the door bangs open, I almost fly off my seat.

"My Lord, Grace, you startled me," says Miss Lesley. "I didn't expect you to be here. But I am glad to see you. We have word from Mr. Hine."

I'm busy hiding the paper so she don't notice the way my letters are leaning, but she's not paying me no mind. She bustles around the room carrying a big yellow envelope.

"Arthur's coming," she says. "He's right behind me."

Soon enough, we're all there, the three of us again, and I'm glad for it. Arthur don't look so sickly. Maybe his mangled hand stops hurting now and again.

Miss Lesley is so excited that we heard from Mr. Hine. She takes care to lock the door and then we settle down around her desk to see what he sent.

First thing she pulls out of the envelope is nothing but a thin skinny book she calls a report. The pictures show kids working in the mill. There's a bobbin-winder boy in a factory and a bunch of kids standing outside and a line of kids going to work. Arthur studies on them for so long that I have to pull the report away from him so I can get a closer look.

"These pictures don't show us," I say. "He didn't send nothing else?"

Miss Lesley pulls out a big notebook and a letter. "This is what he wrote."

I open up the book and smooth down the lined pages. "He promised to send me one of these."

"When?" Arthur asks.

"He left a note on our kitchen table."

Arthur looks mad that I got something and he didn't. "You never told me that."

"Are you two listening?" Miss Lesley says. "The notebook is for both of you."

Now I'm mad. Mr. Hine said he would give me my own notebook, not one I've got to share with Arthur.

She reads.

"Dear Miss Lesley,

As promised, I'm sending you the report we made of mill conditions in the whole of New England. Also, here is a notebook for Grace and Arthur. I would be most grateful if they could write a full description of their daily lives in and out of the mill. Hard facts and details which support what people see in my photographs have proven to be most helpful in convincing the public of the truth of our cause.

Yours cordially,
Lewis Hine"

"He wants us to write in this book?" Arthur asks. "What are we supposed to say?"

"Put down your life before it disappears," I tell him. "That's what he told me." But I am sad too. "Where are my pictures? He promised to send them. There ain't nothing more in that package?"

"That's it, Grace. There *is* nothing more."

"I told you the man don't keep his promises," Arthur growled.

"Doesn't—" says Miss Lesley as usual. I feel sorry for her sometimes. She's never going to change the way we talk.

"Doesn't keep them," interrupts Arthur with an itch in his voice. "I'm not going to write down one word for him."

166

Miss Lesley and I don't look at each other and don't say nothing right away, but we know what Arthur's thinking. He's worried about writing with two fingers missing.

Suddenly I get an idea. I open to the very first page of the notebook. "Well, I'm going to do it," I say. "Watch me, Arthur."

I put the pencil in my left hand and write at the top of the first white page: *The Life of Arthur Trottier As Told by Him to Mr. Lewis Hine*.

All three of us are watching that hand of mine skimming across the paper as if it's got a life of its own, the letters coming out easy and leaning forward like they're running along to catch up with what I'm thinking.

"*Arthur Trottier is twelve years old. He was born on—*"

"December seventh, eighteen ninety-seven," says Arthur, and I write it. Something don't look right.

Miss Lesley tells me, "The *eighteen* needs a *g* in it, Grace."

"You're writing with your left hand," Arthur says out of the blue like he's been studying for a while on what's different about me.

"It's easy, Arthur," I say.

"That's your strong hand. Of course it's easy for you."

He's right. Arthur didn't lose no brains when he lost his fingers.

But I keep going. "We're starting at the beginning. *Arthur was born in Canada,*" I write. "*He moved to America when he was—*"

"Four."

I bet Miss Lesley is itching to change the pencil into my right hand, but she keeps quiet. Finally, she says, "Your letters are nice and even, Grace. Writing with your left hand. I wouldn't have expected that."

We're both tiptoeing along, pretending we ain't one bit interested in Arthur.

"Let me try," he says, and pulls the pencil out of my fingers.

His poor sorry right hand come sliding out of his sleeve like an animal poking its nose from behind a bush. I push the notebook over to his side of the desk. The thumb and the finger take hold of the pencil fine. But when Arthur tries to make the first letter, the pencil flips sideways. He tries two more times, but there ain't nothing but space where there oughta be those backup fingers helping to fix the pencil in its proper place.

Miss Lesley sets it up in Arthur's left hand and curls the fingers around it.

He makes a funny backward A, then an R.

"It takes a while to get used to," I tell him.

"Grace should know," Miss Lesley says in this quiet voice. "According to her, I've been making her use the wrong hand ever since she started writing."

That's right, I think, but I keep my mouth shut. She's saying she's sorry in her own way. That's good enough for me.

By the time Arthur gets through his name, his face is all sweaty. He throws down the pencil. "I can't do it."

"It will take practice," says Miss Lesley. "It's as hard as

learning to walk again. Meanwhile Grace will be our scribe."

"What's a scribe?"

"The person who writes down the story."

Imagine that. Me.

26

MAIL FOR GRACE

There's an envelope sitting on the kitchen table waiting for me when we come in from the mill one night.

"What's that?" Mamère asks.

"Mr. Dupree give it to me," Henry says. "Mail for Grace."

"For Grace?" asks Delia.

Everybody stares at me like I done something wrong again. The only mail we ever get is from family in Canada. They don't write much. And nobody ever wrote me a letter before.

"It must be from Mr. Hine," I say. So see, Arthur, he did keep his promise.

We five slide into our seats around the table as if we're settling down for supper. Everybody's got their eyes on that envelope like it might stand up and walk off if we don't keep watching it.

"It says 'Grace Forcier' right here." Mamère is running her finger across my name in the black ink.

"And 'Lewis Hine' up here in the corner. 'National Child—'" I stop myself. Labor Committee. I should have known that was coming. It's exactly what Mr. Hine wrote at the top of Miss Lesley's envelope.

"Child what?" Mamère asks.

I have to lie. "I can't read the other words. But it come all the way from New York City."

I flip the envelope over quick, but I don't need to worry too much. Mamère is getting pretty good at reading, but not so's she could piece that one out.

Papa hands me a knife. I slit open the top of the envelope and peek inside. There are two pictures. I pull out the first one and look at it, taking my time. When Henry tries to poke his nose in, I push him away with my elbow.

It's me, the same one I saw before, but this time I'm not a ghost girl. My hair is dark and pulled back off my head. My eyes are big and staring right at old Mr. Graflex, just like Mr. Hine told me to do. I'm leaning on Marie still and my left arm looks all skinny and strange, which don't make no sense 'cause that's my strong arm. My big clumsy right hand with the cut on the top hangs down below my pocket, which is bulging out with cotton waste. My feet are black with oil as usual. The smock's got grease spots all over it.

I still have a fearful look on my face like I think Mr. Graflex might gobble me up if I don't watch him every minute. And my eyes have this old-woman worry in them. But you know what? I think I'm kind of pretty too.

The others can't wait no longer. Delia snatches the

171

picture out of my hand and studies it with Papa and Henry looking on. Then she shrugs and hands it to Mamère. Seems like we're all waiting for Mamère and what she's going to say.

She puts out a finger and touches me somewhere on the face. And then before any one of us can stop her, she rips the picture in half and then again and then another time. She goes on ripping while I open my mouth to scream, but no sound comes out.

"Adeline, what are you doing?" my father cries, but by then I am nothing but a heap of shredded, jumbled-up paper on the tablecloth. A piece of my leg is sitting on top of three of Marie's bobbins. One of my big eyes got ripped apart from the other and is staring up at me from the pile.

"That Mr. Hine is a bad man," Mamère says, slapping her palm on top of me, all piled in jagged pieces. "I won't have people seeing Grace in her mill smock. He should have pictured her in her Sunday dress."

I am out of the room before anybody else moves. I am running and running, stumbling over my own feet as I head down the hill. I've got Mr. Hine's envelope pressed close to me and nobody is ever going to get it away from me.

⌣

I've gone into hiding down in Arthur's old place, the tumbledown shack by the river. I don't even know how I got myself there, but there are bramble scrapes across my cheeks 'cause I was moving fast, not caring what snatched out at me from the woods. I'm curled in the corner and I'm talking quiet.

"It's time you come back to get me, Pépé. I'm ready to

go to Canada now. I hate Mamère. She slapped you in the face and now she ripped me in two. I can't doff next to her no more. If you don't come soon, I'm headed upriver on my own to find you."

Someone is saying my name and I start up. But it's not Pépé. It's my father's voice, calling. If I sit quiet, he'll go away.

I'm wrong. He keeps getting closer.

"You here, Grace?"

I don't speak. I don't move.

The door scrapes open past all the summer growth that's pushed up through the rotten floorboards. Papa lifts the lantern high so the light makes its way to me.

"It's time you come home now, Grace."

I shake my head, but I know he's right. I just don't intend to go easy.

He puts a hand to his back, the way he always does when he's changing positions. Then slowly he squats down next to me. "There's something more in that envelope."

I nod.

"What is it?"

"I don't know. There weren't no light to see."

"Let's take a look."

I stare at him.

"I won't touch it, I promise. You can hold it the whole time." He puts the lantern down next to us on the ground and I pull out the last thing left in the envelope.

It's the picture of me and Arthur. This time there's nothing scared about me. It looks as if I'm ready to punch Mr. Graflex right in the middle of his sliding eye. I'm side by side with Arthur with his big old ears flapping and his elbows sticking out. His chin is lifted like he's trying to look older than he is. His hands are resting easy, thumbs caught in the corners of his overalls.

You can see all his fingers.

"Well, don't you look like something," my father says with a wondering sound in his voice. "That's my Grace."

"I'm kind of pretty, ain't I, Papa?"

"I don't know much about pretty. But you do look like someone to be reckoned with. You get that from your mother."

"Don't tell me that," I cry. "Don't."

He lays a hand on my arm. "Your mother's always been a fighter. Sometimes she strikes out without thinking first."

"Like the time she slapped Pépé."

"Yes. That too."

"I miss Pépé. I pretend he's coming back, but I know he ain't."

Papa nods. "Your grandfather was a proud man," he says. "Your mother too. She doesn't want people looking down on us, Grace."

But that don't give her the right to tear me up like that, I think. I don't say it. When he gets to his feet, I go along with him. I keep my hateful thoughts to myself, but it don't mean they're gone away.

⌣

That night after everybody's asleep, I hide my picture with my notebook behind the bureau. Nobody will think to look there.

174

27

MONSIEUR DUPREE

If Mamère is sorry about ripping me into pieces, she don't act it. She's harder than ever on me at the frames. I do what she tells me, but inside I am burning up. I'll make sure nobody ever sees me in a mill-smock picture again, 'cause I won't be wearing one for much longer. I'll find some way to get myself out of this mill. It won't be Arthur's way 'cause I need all my fingers for my writing. But no matter what, I'm going to leave Mamère to do her own doffing. Then what will happen to her hank clock numbers?

—

One day I'm walking out of the mill right on the heels of Mrs. Trottier when French Johnny calls her aside.

"Boy healing well, I see," he says.

She don't speak, but I can see her giving him a look.

"He should be ready to come back in any day now."

"The hand pains him bad," she says.

"He can wrap his fingers round a broom, sure enough. There's always sweeping to be done."

Mrs. Trottier turns on her heel.

"You don't have much more time," French Johnny calls after her.

I know what he's saying. The boy don't work, then no more housing. It's just like Miss Lesley said. The mill finds a way to suck you back in.

We flow out of the building, the whole crowd of us shoulder to shoulder, like a river running down the side of a hill. Some of us peel off to climb the wooden steps to the store, where the doors are always open when the mill closes. As Papa says, we might as well just hand our pay right over to Mr. Dupree at the end of the week, 'cause that's where most of it goes. Seems to me I'm angry at everybody these days and now I've come to understand I'm doffing all those long hours just for Mr. Dupree, I'm noisier than ever with my store counting. It makes the others in line snigger to see him dealing with me and they've taken to pushing me to the front so they can listen.

"Now let's see," I say, licking his pencil and doing my figuring. "The bag of flour is twenty-five cents and the three yards of muslin for my sister, Delia, that's another thirty-five. Five and five is ten, carry the one—"

"You do that on your own time," he growls. "Lots of people in line here. Next."

Mrs. Trottier is standing behind me. "I'll wait," she says in a clear-enough voice. Everybody laughs.

"One and two is three and three is six," I go on. "Sixty cents for today, Mr. Dupree. I'll write the date on that 'cause my papa always wants to know. What day is it?"

"August twenty-seventh, 1910," Mrs. Trottier says. I write it down and fold the paper away into my pocket.

"You watch yourself, missy," Mr. Dupree hisses at me. He leans down close to the counter and I want to take a step back in case spit flies out of his mouth, but I hold my ground. "You and that Miss Lesley of yours are both going to catch trouble."

"Whatever do you mean by that, Monsieur Dupree?" Mrs. Trottier asks, her hand on my arm as a way of saying, I'm right here with you.

"None of your business," he says as he straightens up. "And as for you, Madame Trottier, no, there is no letter for you today. And no more credit neither. Mr. Wilson's cut you off."

I can feel her hand go slack like all the hope for that letter from Mr. Trottier's cousin was caught up inside her finger bones, but her face don't show it. That's what's different about Mrs. Trottier now. She don't show people no more how her troubles might be getting to her.

The line behind us goes silent. We're all of us thinking, Whatever is she going to do now?

"What do you need, Mrs. Trottier?" I ask in a big loud voice, before I can stop myself. "You can put it on our bill. We're close to paid up."

There's a stirring in the room. People are not talking yet, but they're thinking.

"Mr. Dupree, you put a sack of her flour on my bill,"

barks Mr. Donahue from behind us. "My boy Thomas is bringing in good money from the farm."

"She can have some sugar on me," calls Mrs. Vallee from the back of the store.

Some more voices start calling out as if suddenly we all fell into such a miracle time of good fortune that we're richer than the mill owners. Mr. Dupree's got his hands up and he's yelling for quiet, but it ain't doing no good.

—

By the time we get out of there, Mrs. Trottier is so loaded down with supplies, we can't hardly carry them between us.

"Lord, Grace, what do I owe all those people?"

"Don't worry, I put it down," I tell her. "It's here in my pocket."

Mr. Dupree had no choice but to give her what she asked for and Mrs. Trottier made me keep the records. I never had to write so fast and add so much in my head. Mr. Dupree's pencil was worn down to nothing by the time I got done. When I tried to give him back that little stub of a thing, he waved me out of his sight like I was a fly he'd just as soon squish.

I don't think nothing like that ever happened before in the store. Maybe now people will stop thinking that bad luck is a sickness you can catch.

When I open the door to our kitchen figuring on how to tell them what I done, there is such a commotion of noise that nobody even sees me standing there. Mamère and Delia are dancing around arm in arm and Henry's banging a pot in time to my papa's tune on the accordion.

"What's going on?" I yell.

"Papa got his old job back," Henry calls to me. "Loom fixer again starting tomorrow."

Don't take me long to join in. Loom fixer brings in the top pay in the mill. Now the store bill really will get paid off in no time.

28

TROUBLES

When I tell Miss Lesley what Mr. Dupree said to me over the store counter, she shrugs.

"What can he do to me?" But this worried look flashes across her face as if she's trying to figure her way backward to something she might have forgot.

Arthur sits in the corner reading one book after another.

"I can't write down your life if you don't tell me nothing," I say to him.

"What does Mr. Hine care about my life?" he snaps. "Or yours."

"Arthur, learning to write with your left hand will take practice," says Miss Lesley.

"What good's writing gonna do me?"

Miss Lesley never let him talk this way to her before, but ever since his fingers got cut off, she seems confused about what to say to him. I'm not.

"Just 'cause you can't do something perfect right off, you're not gonna even try?" I ask him. "Lucky you never had to doff with the wrong hand all along."

"You're lucky you got two whole hands to doff with."

"You did too," I spit back.

"Grace," says Miss Lesley.

Silence falls down on the room. Even when the truth ain't pretty, I still got to speak it. At least Arthur don't bolt. He just squinches down even lower in his seat.

Feels to me like Arthur's accident broke him into two people. The boy before and the one after. He always had a smart tongue, but he weren't so closed down inside himself the way he is these days. Now he sits in the corner and reads like a rat chewing through feed. No pleasure in it. He just don't know what else to do with himself.

I never did show him the picture of him and me, side by side. It don't feel safe. He'd likely go and rip that one up, considering what he thinks about Mr. Hine. And I'm not letting nobody take that picture away from me.

No letter come for Mrs. Trottier so time's running out on her again. We all bought her stores that one time, but we can't keep on with it. Besides, she told me she's not taking food from her neighbors again without paying them back for the first. And how's she going to do that?

These days my mind jumps so quick from one trouble to the next. It feels like a whole row going down at once and I've got to scurry along and piece up all the ends that are flying around every which way. Only thing that concentrates my brain is writing our life history. I'm all the way through Arthur's life and halfway done with mine. Maybe

Mr. Hine don't care a thing about us no more like Arthur says, but it give me something to do. Once it's done and corrected, Miss Lesley says she'll send it to Mr. Hine to show to his committee.

She sits at her desk, getting the lessons ready for the next week. Arthur chews on his books and I write. The weather's cooling down already, halfway into September. It's quiet in the schoolroom. Every so often when I ask Miss Lesley how to spell a certain word, she speaks out the letters without looking up from her work. I pretend that this is my real job, sitting in the quiet, writing all day without having to run my feet off chasing bobbins.

Before I hear any steps, a shadow moves across the slant of light in the doorway behind me. I must be going deaf from six days a week in the spinning room.

"Good afternoon, Madame Forcier," says Miss Lesley, staring right over my head.

Mamère here? I don't look up or turn around.

"I come for Arthur. His mother needs him."

"I see you brought my book. If you're all done with it, I could lend you another."

"I can read all the words in this one now," she says.

"You didn't tell me that," I say, whipping around.

"I've been studying on my own at night," she says, not paying me no mind. "With no help."

I turn back to my work while Miss Lesley goes through the pile of books on her desk.

"This is the level-two reader," she says, handing over the green one. "Henry's on number four, but it won't be long before you catch up with him."

182

Mamère takes the book and peers at the front cover. She handles it careful like it might break if she drops it.

"Why don't you look around?" Miss Lesley says. "It won't bother any of us."

"I just come to tell Arthur his mother's looking for him," Mamère says, but I can see her starting around the room. Her fingers trail across the bookshelf, then up over the blackboard. Miss Lesley jumps up and writes *Madame Forcier* on the board. "You try it," she says, holding out the piece of chalk.

"She ain't learned the writing yet, just the letters," I say quick.

I might as well be a desk, for all the notice they pay me.

"Try the *F*."

My mother picks up the chalk, turns it round and round in her fingers and then sniffs it. Her first line down the board makes a nasty squeak and she jumps back as if something bit her.

"Slant it a little," says Miss Lesley.

She does know how to make the letter *F* and then the *O*. She's just puzzling over the *R* with Miss Lesley on the side waiting for her to work it out when we hear more steps. Mr. Wilson and then Mr. Dupree push their way into the schoolroom, both of them trying to fit through the door at once.

"What's going on here?" barks Mr. Wilson.

"Extra lessons," says Miss Lesley. There are two pink spots, one on each of her cheeks. "No rules against that as far as I know, Mr. Wilson."

I close my notebook up quick and slide it away out of

sight. Arthur can't get no lower in his corner. My mother steps away from the board and slaps her hands once or twice the way she does on baking day to dust off the bread flour.

"Where's the boy?" Mr. Wilson says.

"Over there," says Mr. Dupree, who's been poking around all the time he's been in the room. Who give him permission?

"Boy, you go on out of here now," Mr. Wilson orders. "You and your mother are moving on."

"Where?" I ask, but they don't look at me.

"That's why I come down here," my mother says to Arthur. "To fetch you."

That's not true. Mamère never went to fetch nobody. She would have sent Henry or Delia. Or me if I'd been around. Arthur was just an excuse so she could get that next reader from Miss Lesley.

"Did my mother get her letter?" Arthur asks, standing up.

There's no mail on Sunday, Arthur, I want to tell him. But I keep quiet.

"I don't know about any letter, son," says Mr. Wilson. "All I know is your mother says she won't let you work in the mill, not even as a sweeper. That means you two are moving along. Time you give up the house for some real workers. Way past time."

"You can't do that," says Miss Lesley in her sure voice. "You can't throw people out as if they're nothing but trash."

"They've been warned and warned, miss. They've got to be out by tomorrow. New family coming in on the train."

184

Arthur is making his way through the desks slowly. He looks at me, but we don't say nothing out loud with our mouths. It's finally happened, his eyes say. Where will you go, my eyes ask. He don't have no answer.

"I'll go along with you, Arthur," Miss Lesley says, moving to catch up with him. "I want to speak to your mother."

But Mr. Wilson hooks her by the arm as she tries to pass him by. "Not so quick, miss. I've got business with you too."

Then suddenly I know what Mr. Dupree is doing here, sneaking around the corners of the room, looking at us out of the sides of his eyes.

"Miss Lesley didn't do nothing wrong," I cry. "You leave her alone." And I go for Mr. Wilson, but Mamère grabs me as I fly by and pulls me right up close against her.

"Who is that girl?" Mr. Wilson asks.

Miss Lesley has stood off from him. "Take her out," she says to my mother in a low voice. "Go on quickly. Grace, you keep quiet for once, you hear? I'll talk to you later."

"*Tais-toi*," my mother spits in my ear.

She has strong muscles in her hands from years of cranking up the builder. Her fingers are wrapped so tight around the top of my arm that I'll be showing a bruise by morning.

That's the way we go up French Hill, her dragging me along behind like I'm nothing but some cart bumping over the rocks. We're all the way inside the kitchen before she finally lets me go.

"What is it?" Papa says.

185

"They're throwing the Trottiers out," says my mother. "I warned that woman and warned her again. The boy could have done the sweeping. And Grace here was fixing to kill the overseer."

I don't say nothing. All I know is I've got to see Arthur before he goes.

29

GOODBYE

Nobody tries to stop me when I say I'm going to the
Trottiers'. My father nods and my mother says, "Take her
this." She hands me a sack with a loaf of bread and some
sausage. "It's not much, but they'll need food for the trip.
Wherever she's going." I'm staring at Mamère. "Get along
with you, Grace," she snaps. "They'll be halfway down
French Hill by the time you get there."

At the last minute, I decide to take the picture of me
and Arthur standing together so I can show it to him. I
won't let him touch it, but he needs to see himself whole
again. This is what you look like, Arthur. Two fingers don't
matter much. You still got everything else.

They're collected at the front door of their house, sharing out the bundles. Two people can't carry much between them. Arthur's got a sack over his shoulder and I can tell it's all books from the way the corners of them are poking at the burlap just like they're fighting to get out and get read.

"Miss Lesley's been here," he says the moment he sees me.

"Hello, Grace," says Mrs. Trottier.

"My mother sent you this." I hand over the sack. "Food for the trip."

"She is kind. I won't be able to pay everybody back," she says with a fussing look on her face.

"We'll do without," I say.

"Miss Lesley give us the train fare as far as New Hampshire. We're going to find Mr. Trottier's cousin."

"Miss Lesley's leaving too," says Arthur. "Mr. Wilson threw her out 'cause she brought in Mr. Hine."

"You're lying," I spit, but inside myself I know it's true. The minute I saw snaky Mr. Dupree sliding around the edges of our classroom, I knew what he was there for. How is it that whole months can go by with nothing changing and then in this one day, I'm losing Arthur and Miss Lesley and my Sunday schooling? But I know I've got to stop the thinking about all that right now 'cause Arthur and Mrs. Trottier are lifting their bundles and there's not much time.

"I've got something to show you," I tell him.

"I'll go on ahead," Mrs. Trottier says. "Train's not due for an hour. You take care of yourself, Grace."

She puts her bundles down again and pulls me against her so my nose is smashed right into the old mill smell caught up in the cloth of her gray dress and the envelope

188

I'm holding is pressed between us. Then just as quick, she lets me go and starts down the hill.

"*Bon voyage*, Madame Trottier," I call after her, and she waves one free hand, her body still leaning forward away from French Hill and this old mill house where nothing much good ever happened to her.

I lead Arthur back inside the kitchen. Someone else will be sleeping in here tomorrow night. I can stand Arthur not being in the mill with me, back to back sliding down the rows between our frames. I'm used to missing his eyes watching me between the spindles on cleaning day. But now even on Sundays there's going to be a huge hole where Arthur and Miss Lesley used to be. Like the hole Pépé left in the corner of our kitchen. And that one's still not filled. How many people do I got to give up?

"What you brought to show me?" he asks.

I can't wait no more. The light is fading and the lantern on the table is empty of kerosene.

I slide the photograph out, keeping a safe distance from him. "Mr. Hine sent me this picture," I tell him. "You and me."

He just looks and looks like he can't believe that's him staring back. I know what he's looking at. That whole complete hand of his hanging off the pocket of his overalls, same ones he's wearing now.

"I thought you should see yourself like this before you leave."

He reaches out to take it, but I yank it away quick. "No touching. Mamère ripped up my other one."

"Why'd she do that?"

189

I shrug. "She don't want people seeing me in my mill smock."

"You look like you're fixing to fight someone," he says.

"It's only two fingers, Arthur. You still got everything else."

For once, he don't give no smart answers. He just keeps on looking like he's trying to make the picture stay in his brain. And right then and there, before I can change my mind, I decide to give him his half.

"You got your knife?"

He nods.

"Get it out," I order, and I lay the picture flat on the table.

"What're you fixing to do?"

"Watch me."

I fold the paper and slit it down the middle. We're still side by side, but now there's a line dividing us. It gives me an ache to see that.

"Here, take it," I tell him, holding out his half.

"How about I take you and you keep me?" he says. "So's we don't forget."

I know what he means, and for a second, I think he's right. We could hold on to each other that way. But then I shake my head. "I won't forget what you look like," I say. "But now I've got me, I can't let go. I can't. And you need to do that too."

He don't argue, but takes the picture of his old cocky self and slides it between the pages of one of those books of his.

I put my half back in the envelope and I know the

190

goodbye is coming right at us and I'd just as soon jump over it.

"Don't miss your train," I say, and start up the hill to my house 'cause my throat is shutting down like it's choked with lint.

"I'll write you a letter," he shouts. "With my left hand."

"You better," I shout back. My voice croaks.

But I don't let myself turn around and look at him one more time. I'm practicing keeping the picture of him in my head.

30

MISS LESLEY

Not letting yourself cry is a lot of work. It tires me out and now I just want to slip through the back window of our house and curl up in bed next to Delia.

I lean through and drop my envelope down behind the bureau.

The lantern's still lit in the kitchen and there are people talking around the table. I slip along the edge of the porch to listen. Seems Miss Lesley has marched herself up French Hill one more time.

"It's not enough," my mother is saying. "Cuts her pay by fifty cents a week."

"I've told you all this before, Mrs. Forcier." Miss Lesley's voice sounds dull and tired. "You know how I feel about Grace's schooling. I've given up all my free Sundays to come in and teach her along with Arthur. I won't be here anymore and you can be sure the next teacher won't be bothering. A teacher can make as much as twenty dollars a week. This would give her a real chance to get out of the mill."

"What chance?" I ask, stepping through the door.

The three of them look up at me, but it's Henry's voice from the corner that speaks first.

"She wants you to be the teacher."

"Not the teacher exactly, Henry," says Miss Lesley. "A substitute just until the new one comes. The pay would be two dollars a week for now. I got Mr. Wilson to agree to offer you the position temporarily. He was in such a rush to fire me, he hadn't figured out who would be coming to take my place. It'll be a month or two before he finds someone. You could be teacher till then. Meanwhile you could be studying for the Normal School exam."

"We can't give up the extra money now," says Mamère, standing up to make herself more sure of what she's saying. "Just when we're getting caught up."

"Papa has his old job back," I say. Imagine being a teacher. Me. Even for a little while.

Delia is leaning against the doorframe of our room. "Grace ain't such a good doffer, Mamère." When I open my mouth to snap at her, I catch her wink. "Valerie's fast. With Mrs. Trottier gone, Valerie could take Grace's place on your frames."

"No," says Papa. He rarely speaks up, but this time he backs my mother. "We are grateful to you, miss, but Grace works in the mill as a doffer. That's her job. If she were to come out of there, we might lose this house."

"But don't you see?" Miss Lesley cries. "Grace would

still be working for the mill owners. Remember, they own the school and run it. And pay the teachers."

There's a little silence while she gets to her feet. "I give up," she says with a shrug. Me and Henry have heard her say that before in the classroom, but this time she sounds like she really means it. "I am sick and tired of wanting more for your children than you people want for them yourselves. I'm done."

"Will we have school tomorrow?" Henry asks. He wants to go so's he can show off the new shoes Mamère bought him yesterday at the store. His first pair ever.

"I don't expect so, Henry," Miss Lesley says. "Nobody to teach you. I'll be gone by noon."

"Where will you go?" I ask.

"I have a sister who works in the mills down in North Adams. Right across the border in Massachusetts."

"Père Alain's sister lives in a convent in North Adams."

Miss Lesley nods. "I'll move in with my sister and her husband for now. Who knows, Grace? Maybe I'll be doffing myself before long."

"No doffing down in that mill, miss," my father says. "It's called Arnold Print Works. It's where our cloth goes to be printed."

The way she stares at my father, I can see she didn't hear a word he said. Her eyes are getting all shiny. I don't know who she feels saddest about—me or her or Arthur. Or the whole collection of us that spent so many Sundays huddled round those desks together.

The train whistle blows. "There goes Arthur," I say, looking at her.

"Walk me down the hill," she says, holding out her hand. I'm too big to be holding somebody's hand, but I take hers.

"Grace, you got that laundry downstairs to hang out," my mother says, but I pretend I don't hear.

"Goodbye, Mrs. Forcier," says Miss Lesley. "I hope you're able to keep up your reading. You too, Henry."

"Thank you, miss," my father says, but we don't look at him. Suddenly, I don't like the family God give me. Me and Miss Lesley walk out the door together. If we started running right then, I bet we could make it onto Arthur's train.

But I know I can't twist together a new family the way I make cotton thread from a bunch of flying ends. Miss Lesley has her sister. Arthur and his mother got each other. I can't make them stay with me.

At the bottom of the hill, she pulls my notebook out of her bag. "You put that somewhere safe."

I hug it up close to me. "I give Arthur a picture Mr. Hine made of him. It shows him with both his fingers."

"What will become of Arthur?" she asks out loud, but I know she's not 'specting me to come up with the answer. She's talking to God or the wind or the trees.

"He should have gone to Massachusetts. You said they don't let kids like us work in the mills down there."

"I told Mrs. Trottier that, but she is so sure that this cousin is going to help them. He lives in Manchester, New Hampshire."

"How far away is that?" I ask.

"Other side of Vermont and then north. The Coolidge mill in that town has got one of the biggest spinning rooms in the world. Arthur and his mother are going from the frying pan into the fire."

I don't know what she's talking about and she can tell. She give herself a little shake. "Grace, I tucked Mr. Hine's address in the front of your notebook. When you finish your life story, you find a way to get it to him. But don't you mail it from here. Not with Mr. Dupree watching everything you do."

"You wouldn't be leaving if Mr. Hine had never come."

"You're right, Grace. Sometimes people trying to do good can make trouble all their own without thinking. I never should have pushed Arthur as hard as I did."

I don't have no answer for that.

"Did you read my book?" I ask.

"I did. Your handwriting's clear enough even though the letters lean the wrong way." I open my mouth, but she goes right on. "I marked the spelling errors and corrected the grammar."

I wait for more. Finally it comes.

"You've got your own particular writing style, Grace. It sounds just like you."

"Is that bad?"

She smiles a little. "No, it's fine."

"Did Mr. Wilson really say I could be the teacher?"

"A substitute. Just until he finds someone else. It would be a start for you." She shivers as if suddenly she's cold. Then she takes me by the shoulders. "But it's for your mother and father to say. Don't get foolish ideas in your head, Grace, the way Arthur did. You pay attention to those bobbins, you hear me?"

I say yes, but I don't intend to.

"Off I go, then." Her voice sounds brisk the way it always did when she was ordering me to sit back down at my desk.

"Arthur says he'll write to me."

"Letters got us in this trouble in the first place," she says.

"But I'm the only one left behind," I shout, and it snatches the top off the bottle of tears that I thought were all stopped up inside.

She hunches down in front of me and tries wiping them away, fast as they come. I expect the ink off her fingers is leaving black streaks on my face. "I know, Grace," she says. "I'll write. I promise." Seems to me that crying scares her as much as me 'cause suddenly she tucks some scrunched-up piece of paper in my smock pocket and she's gone, scrambling down the last bit of the hill to the main road.

I watch long as I can, but the dark rubs out the sight of her in her blue dress before she even turns the corner. When I get home, I unfold the paper and read it by the light of a candle. It tells me her address in North Adams. So she do mean me to write her.

Delia's sprawled across the whole bed. Even though she don't wake up, her body knows to move over and make room for me when I slide under the blanket.

31

THE SMOCK

With all the confusion of the day, I never did get my clothes hung up to dry. In the morning Delia takes pity on me and gives me her old smock to wear. Most summer days I don't bother with my drawers 'cause there's nothing worse than standing by your frame with wet clothes sticking to your skin. But Delia's smock is big on me and flaps around, which means I've got to borrow Henry's extra union suit off the line and pull that on underneath.

My mother and father busy themselves around the kitchen. Nobody's looking at me and nobody's talking. We all manage to get out of the house without saying a word to one another. Henry comes to the mill with us 'cause word's gone around town that the schoolroom will stay locked until further notice.

The wind is up. Vermont in September gives you warnings, says, Remember what I've got in store for you. I wish

I'd put on my coat like Delia, but I always leave the house in a jumble. She's so different from me. Some nights she even lays out her smock as if she's a fancy girl with three to choose from and what a bother it would be fussing over which one to wear in the morning.

We walk past Arthur's house on the way down the hill. The front door is standing open like someone just took a quick trip to the store. Someone who thought they'd be coming back shortly. I wonder where Arthur is by now. Did he get to Manchester yet? Did they find that cousin? Is he going to have to go right back into a mill?

~

French Johnny sends Valerie over to doff for Delia, which is a good thing for us Forciers 'cause it means Delia's hank clock numbers will be up. But he don't give Delia Mrs. Trottier's machines, which makes Mamère really mad. Lunch break she grumbles about it.

"Everybody knows those machines are better than Delia's. He needs to move her over."

Nobody says nothing for a minute and then Madame Cordeau calls out, "You got the six best frames in the room already, Adeline. How much more you want?"

"And that girl of yours is getting ahead of herself," calls someone else. I don't see who. "Why does she get schooling on Sunday?"

"It's 'cause of her the teacher got fired," says another. I'm keeping my head down. "The way she makes trouble with Dupree."

Everybody's stirring and putting their eyes here and there, but not looking at my mother. People can turn on you so fast when they're all bunched up together. It happens just the same way with my frames when one end flies off and gives the next one ideas.

"Somebody says now you're learning yourself to read," says Mrs. Donahue.

"What's wrong with that?" Mamère demands. "Any one of you could try it. And your children could have gone on Sundays. Miss Lesley didn't set a limit on numbers."

Wouldn't Miss Lesley be surprised to hear this, I think. My mother standing up for her.

The grumbling settles down after that, but there's no singing at break. Come to think of it, there ain't been none for a while.

—

I can't believe it's the beginning of the week and I've got six days to plow through. My feet are already pounding, but my head is misbehaving even worse. I can't make my brain stay satisfied with bobbin counting. It keeps wandering off to Arthur and then to Miss Lesley. Is she all packed up by now? How's she getting down to that sister's house? Does the sister know she's coming? Will Miss Lesley really end up in a mill? How can that be?

If I'd been paying mind I would have felt that first warning tug, the only pinch of time you got to pull yourself out. Once I figure what's happening, I'm getting turned round from front to back by bad old Edwin, who's snatched a flapping piece of my big borrowed smock and is gobbling it right up.

"Mamère," I scream. "Mamère!"

Edwin keeps on munching and I'm facing front now but getting pulled back against the frame with the buzzing spindles moving closer and closer. I scream again and suddenly a whole wall of Mamère presses into my face and she is reaching right over my head to throw the shipper handle. Finally the buzzing stops just inches from my ears.

I'm all twisted up in the machine with my back pressed hard against the clearing board. The tops of the spindles are digging into me something bad and the blouse under my smock is cutting into my neck.

"Get me out!" I scream.

"Hush, Grace, it's all right," my mother says, but her eyes look wide and scared. She reaches in behind and starts hauling on my smock to drag it out from between the gears, but Edwin is hanging on just as tight. It feels like they're two dogs fighting over me and I ain't nothing but a bone.

"Mamère, stop," I cry out. "You're choking me."

"Leave her be," says French Johnny's voice. "I'll cut her out."

It hurts to move my head, but when he passes in front of me, I see he's got a big old knife out in the open.

"You be careful, Johnny," my mother warns.

"Step away now, Adeline. I need to get in there beside her."

My mother don't move. "I'll do the cutting," she says.

"Adeline, you listen to me. I've done this before. Get out of my way."

She finally moves around so her face is right in front where I can see her.

"You stand very still, Grace, and nothing will happen," she says to me. But it don't sound much like she believes it. And where does she think I'm going anyway? I'm trying hard as I can to put some distance between me and that bad old Edwin, but my feet can't keep themselves straight on the oily floor.

"For mercy's sake, girl, stop moving around," mutters French Johnny. "I don't want to cut you." He smells like sweat and grease and smoke all at once. I shut my eyes to try and think of something else. I wish I could hold my nose too, but Edwin's pinned me bad enough so I can't move my arms.

The knife saws its way through the smock from just behind my knees and up my back where the cloth's pulled in the tightest. I suck in my breath and hold it to give French Johnny all the space he needs to slip that blade past my shoulder bones.

The bottom part of me comes free, which means my feet start to slide out in the grease. French Johnny puts his arm around my waist to hold me up and now I think I'm really going to be sick all over him and myself what with the smell and the feeling of his arm passing over my front like that. But the top part of me is still caught fast and there's only an inch between my neck and the frame.

"Damn, girl," whispers French Johnny. His hot breath tickles me right in the ear like he's telling me some secret. "You really did this one up fine."

The knife is worked in so close I can hear it chomping away, one little cloth bite after another.

"Ouch," I yell when the point pokes me in the back of the head. It ain't nothing but a pinprick, but I'm making sure French Johnny knows how close he is.

"Johnny," cries Mamère.

And then suddenly with no warning, the knife makes its way through to air right behind my neck and I fall forward against French Johnny's arm and my feet are scrambling down below trying their best to be holding me up. My back and my legs are bare, open to the air and all the eyes in the room.

"Now look at this," roars French Johnny over the noise of the frames. "This crazy girl's wearing her brother's drawers." I yell and squirm away. Then I hear a slap but for once it don't land on me.

"You leave her be, Johnny." There's a growl in Mamère's voice I never heard before. She twirls me around and backs me up against her so nobody else can see.

Behind French Johnny, the torn-away half of Delia's smock is hanging out from between the spindles like a piece of meat in a dog's mouth. And beyond that down the row, people are staring.

"You had no cause to do that," French Johnny mutters, rubbing the red mark on his cheek.

"Grace, you all right?" asks Mamère, and this time it's her voice in my ear.

"Course she is, Adeline," he answers for me. "I made sure that knife never touched her." For once he don't got that blustery voice of his. He sounds shamed.

"I thank you for that," my mother says, each word careful as it goes past my ear. If nobody else gives away that they

203

saw what happened, then there's a chance the slap will be one of those pretend secrets we all keep and he won't have to punish her. After all, she's still the best spinner he's got and that counts for a lot. By the time he turns around to check the room, everybody's back to their spinning as if their eyes never lifted from their frames.

"Go on, Johnny, and leave us be," Mamère says. "My frames need to be shut down."

"That girl of yours is more trouble than ten others," he says. But he goes.

—

"Mamère," says Delia's voice. "Grace can wear my coat."

I'm beginning to shake a little, which is strange 'cause now it's all over. But it feels like my body's not really part of me at this moment. It's taking its own time getting through to the other side of this.

Mamère is still holding me against her, but I know everybody's seen me lying across French Johnny's arm with my backside showing. It'll just be a matter of time before Dougie or Felix starts tormenting me about Henry's union suit. The snickering will jump from their mouths to someone else's until it runs right around the mill and on into the town.

"Hold your arms out," Delia tells me, and I do what she says.

"Things in a mess?" Mamère asks as the two of them wrap me in the coat. I feel like a package getting bundled up for mailing.

"Bad enough," Delia says. "I got to two of yours before the clearing boards went. But the rest are down. And so are mine."

What she's saying is, we've got an hour of piecing up before we can start the frames. An hour off the hank clocks.

"Go along home, Grace," my mother says, but her voice shakes a little. "You can walk?"

I nod. It's not the walking that bothers me. It's all the eyes watching as I pass.

"I'll take you to the stairs," says Delia. Sometimes it torments me that Delia seems to know what I'm thinking without me telling her. This time I'm grateful.

Mamère comes too. They put me between them and we cross the room that way. They don't exactly carry me, but they make a wall around me until I'm safe in the stairwell.

"I'm fine now," I say, my hand on the railing.

"Take your time coming back," Mamère says.

Coming back, I think. I ain't never coming back.

When I turn around and look, they're both still there watching me make my way down the steps.

Au revoir, I say without speaking out loud. I'm already adding them to the pictures of people I carry in my head. Arthur, Miss Lesley—now my whole family.

32

ACROSS THE BORDER

By the time I get inside our front door, I've made up my mind. I'm going to North Adams, where they won't let kids my age work in the mills. Maybe I can board in with Miss Lesley or I can stay in the convent with Père Alain's sister. Just until I find work. Maybe I can piece together a new family for myself after all.

Shaky as I am, it don't take me long to pull things together. What have I got, after all? One damp smock and some underwear that I put on, my Sunday dress, the shoes passed down from Delia, a winter coat, my notebook, my photograph, my sister Claire's birth paper from the trunk in case I need to prove I'm fourteen. After all, fourteen-year-olds get hired as teachers.

Mamère never could really count on me, I think as I bundle my things together. I'm not regular and easy like

Delia, satisfied with spinning, looking to make it to the weaving room. I've got my clumsy right hand and my jumpy brain and my big mouth making smart with Mr. Dupree. It will be better for the rest of them when I'm gone. Life will ease along without so much trouble. And now there'll only be four around the table looking to eat.

But I don't want to be thinking about them too much. I've got to hurry if I'm going to catch the southbound mail train that comes through at noon.

—

A long time before the engine turns the corner, the rails begin to shiver. I'm standing by the tracks a ways south of the station where nobody will think to look for me. I've been real clever, dodging through the woods and hunkering down low when I pass under Mr. Dupree's window. I plan to swing myself up onto the first freight car behind the engine. I'll have plenty of time 'cause they take a while unloading the mail and the store supplies.

I know what I'm doing, I keep telling myself. I'm not like Pépé, who was wandering through the woods, crazy in his head. But my legs are still shaking, bad as the rails.

The train turns the corner, the brakes scream and it slows to a stop. I picked the right place 'cause I only have to trot a little ways back toward the station to get to the first freight car.

But the sliding door is only open a half foot and I know I don't have the strength to budge it. The crack is so narrow

I can barely push my bundle into the car. Finally it pops through and then it's my body's turn. Lucky I don't got no extra fat on my bones.

The mail is all unloaded, but Mr. Dupree is chatting with one of the engineers. When I'm sure they ain't looking my way, I swing myself up and get my head and shoulders through the opening. But then I stick, halfway in and halfway out.

"Come on, Grace, come on." My smock catches on a nail at the edge of the door and I can't work my hand back to free it. If Mr. Dupree takes one look this way, he's going to see a couple of legs sticking out in the air, waving at him.

Suddenly I hear shouting from down the line and the train begins to roll ever so slowly. I did it. I'm going to make it, even if my hips are caught in the opening as tight as my smock was in the spinning frame. But it don't matter. Now the train's moving, I've got time to slide my hand back, free the smock and inch myself inside. Once we get to the next station, I'll be safe.

Just as I manage to work another inch of myself inside, there's more shouting and the brakes squeal again and the train slows and stops. What now? I force myself to lie still and wait with my legs pulled up as close as they can be. The voices come nearer and then seem to pass right by.

"Where?"

"Maybe it's nothing."

I'm holding my breath. The wind comes up. The train whistle blows once, but still we don't move. My cheek is pressed against the floorboards of the car. From the smell, I can tell the last thing it carried was horses.

I'm praying to Pépé. I've given up on God. "Pépé, get

me out of here. Get me somewhere safe. I can't be in that mill no more."

But I'm not so sure that Pépé is going to answer my prayers. "Grace," he's saying. "You're leaving your family?"

Then with a roar, the door slides open and the sun pours in. I pull up my legs and rub the scrapes. I can't see nothing in the sudden light.

"Just like you thought, Mr. Dupree," says a man's voice. "We got ourselves a stowaway."

"Bring her on out of there. Foolish girl. You'd think she'd know better. Her grandfather got killed by a train not three months ago."

I never do see the man who helps me out of the car, but he holds me tight by the arms when he passes me like a sack down to Mr. Dupree.

—

Mamère come to get me. That's the worst part. I wish they'd sent Delia or Papa. But she's the one. More time on the loose pulley all 'cause of me.

She takes my bundle, nods to Mr. Dupree and walks me up the hill. We don't say a word the whole way.

When she sits me down at the table, I open my mouth, but she shakes her head.

"For once in your life, Grace, be still and listen. I don't have much time and Lord knows, I don't have the strength for arguments. I told French Johnny to give me Valerie to doff. You can do as Miss Lesley says. You can be the teacher until Mr. Wilson finds the next one."

I can't believe what I'm hearing. "What about the fifty cents?"

"We'll do without for now. You study for that test Miss Lesley wants you to take. Teachers who pass that test make good money, she told me. Better than you can make doffing. Almost as good as the weavers."

"What about when the new teacher comes? Will I have to go back in the mill?"

"Grace, I can't tell you what will happen then."

"I ain't going back in the mill, Mamère. I ain't never going back there. If I have to, I'll run away again."

"Don't speak to me like that, Grace. You'll do what you're told."

"Yes, Mamère."

"All I know is you're better at reading and numbers than you'll ever be at doffing."

I know she'll think I'm acting smart, but I speak up anyway. "And you're better at spinning than you ever were at farming, right, Mamère?"

She starts and lifts her hand to cuff me, but then her face breaks into a smile 'cause my words do make sense to her.

"Yes," she says at last, "I 'spect I am."

"You think I'll make a good teacher, Mamère?" I ask, shoring myself up against the harsh words that could come.

She studies on her answer for a while. "You taught me just fine, Grace. I'm already catching up to Henry with my reading."

I grin inside. Mamère was my first student. I wonder how many more there'll be.

We sit together awhile longer, acting like there's no hank clock waiting. Just a girl and her mother with nothing special to do.

But she gets to her feet before long. "Clean yourself up before you start the supper."

"Yes, Mamère."

In the doorway, she turns around. "Your Pépé would be happy, Grace. He hated you working in the mill."

Later on, I think it's all come around in a big circle. Mamère letting me out of the mill makes up for that slap she landed on Pépé's cheek. And if Pépé's in heaven, then maybe he knows I'm not working in the mill no more.

33

FIRST DAY

I wake with the mill bell, but when I put my hand out to snatch my smock off the hook, it ain't there.

Delia's laid out my Sunday dress.

"First day you wear this," she says, moving around our bed in the early-morning dark. "You need to show them who's boss. I figure after today, you can use your old school pinafore."

Ain't that just like Delia, worrying about my clothes?

My stomach don't take well to the cornmeal mush Mamère sets in front of me, but I manage to choke down a piece of bread dipped in hot coffee.

We all leave together, except for Henry, who will be coming along with the other children when I ring the school bell. At the turning to the mill, the four of us stop 'cause for the first time in months, I've got to go a different way. The others streaming down the hill give us room.

"You make those kids behave, Grace," shouts Mrs.

Cordeau as she sweeps past, and that starts up a lot of joking and carrying on from the rest of them. "Use that ruler, Grace." "Don't let my girl get away with nothing." "Make Pierre carry in the wood when the weather turns."

I smile, knowing they mean well. We ain't never had a Franco teacher before and they're showing they're proud of me. But it don't help settle my stomach. What made me think I could do this?

Mamère takes my face in her two hands and I feel the rough skin of her palms against my cheeks. She looks at me straight without saying nothing, but it's a kind of blessing that she's giving me. Then they're all three of them gone, Papa, Mamère, Delia, running to slip through the big iron gates just before they swing shut.

The schoolroom feels like it's been holding its breath, waiting for something or someone to start it up again. I stand inside the front door, taking in the smell of chalk and book dust and woodsmoke from last week's fire, the first of the season.

I shut my eyes and for one minute, I can see Arthur at the desk we shared and Miss Lesley at hers. I remember the day Mr. Hine took my picture and how the flash left that ghostly shadow of him standing in a place he'd already moved away from. I wonder how long it will be before I come in this room and don't see their shadows waiting on me.

My mother's writing is still up on the board. With the chalk slanted proper in my left hand, I draw a tail on the *R* she started and finish up the name. Then I put a *Miss* in front of it. That's what a new teacher always does first thing. Writes her name on the board.

I circle the desk twice and then lower myself onto the stool. Lucky it's high up 'cause it makes me look older and taller than I am. Miss Lesley has left the new teacher a pile of books and supplies. A folded note under the inkwell's got my name penned on it in her even, proper handwriting.

Grace, it says. *I hope you are the one reading this*. Then she give me a list of the students and what level reader they're using and what writing assigments each one can handle. Underneath that she's left me the studying book for the Normal School certification test. I can see by the pages she's marked that I'm only halfway through the lessons I've got to know to pass.

I get a dizzy feeling when I see all the books snuggled up tight against one another on the shelves under the blackboard. Miss Lesley never did let any of us get near those shelves, not even Arthur. She handed the books out and dusted them and put them away herself. But now I'm the keeper of the books. I hunker down to read the names.

Spenser's *Faerie Queene*, *Marjorie's Busy Days*, all the Appleton Readers in a row except for the one Mamère is working on, something called the *Iliad* by a man with just one name, and *The Red Badge of Courage*. Twenty-two books in all.

In the distance, I hear voices. I jump. How much time has gone by?

I carry in a bucket of water and lay out the readers, one on every third desk. Moving around calms my brain the way it always does.

214

Then it's time. I go out to the porch and haul on the rope. The metal tongue smacks the iron wall of the bell above my head once, twice, three times.

"School's in session," I say to myself as I see little Ora Vallee, my first student, turn the corner at the bottom of French Hill.

One week later, I send my notebook to Mr. Hine with this letter. Now I'm the teacher, I've been paying attention to my grammar so I do the letter over three times to be sure it's right.

September 22, 1910

> *Dear Mr. Hine,*
> *This is the notebook you wanted me and Arthur to fill up. I had to do all the writing. Arthur cut off two of his fingers when he caught them in a frame and he couldn't hold the pencil after that. He left town with his mother and Miss Lesley got fired and I'm the teacher for now. It's not easy, but it's better than the mill.*
> *Thank you for the pictures.*
> *Your friend,*
> *Grace Forcier*

more of the story

Photograph on pages 216–217:
All these children worked in the North Pownal Cotton Mill in 1910. Addie, the girl in the photograph on the book jacket, on the title page, and on page 222, is in the front row. She's leaning on the girl to her left, probably her older sister, Annie. Photograph by Lewis Hine.

ABOUT LEWIS HINE

Lewis Hine was born in Oshkosh, Wisconsin, on September 26, 1874. His father died the year he graduated from high school. To help support the family, Hine went to work in an upholstery factory thirteen hours a day, six days a week, for four dollars a week. After seven years of working at jobs that he hated, he met a professor of education who convinced him to take evening classes at the state Normal School. In 1901, Hine moved to New York City to teach at the Ethical Culture School, where he became the school photographer. His students there remembered him fondly as a mime and a trickster. These acting skills served him well in later years when he needed to talk his way inside the mills.

In 1904, Hine took his camera to Ellis Island to photograph the streams of immigrants eager to find a new life in America. Perhaps because of his own early experiences at dull, dead-end jobs, Hine was particularly horrified by the idea of child labor. So it was natural for this young photographer to follow the trail of those newly arrived families as they made their way into the city streets and factories and cotton fields of America looking for work. In 1907, Hine traveled to Pittsburgh to document the lives of laborers in an industrial city. "We live underneath America," a steel-worker said. "America goes on above our heads."

In 1908, Hine left teaching to take a job as staff photographer for the National Child Labor Committee. He was paid one hundred dollars a month.

Hine did whatever he could to get the pictures of child workers. Sometimes he told the mill foreman he was selling postcards or Bibles. Other times he pretended that he had been ordered by someone in the head office to photograph the machinery. If he could not get into a mill, he photographed the workers walking home at the end of their thirteen-hour day. And everywhere he went, he took notes as well as pictures because he knew that without concrete evidence, the mill owners would denounce his photographs as fakes. Child labor was cheap and the owners needed children to work in their mills to keep their costs down and their shareholders happy. Superintendents, inspectors and often the parents, desperate for that extra bit of income, all pretended that the children were happy at their work and the conditions were healthy and safe.

But Hine knew better. He once said, "I have always been more interested in persons than in people." With a kind word and a smile, he showed the children that they could trust him. He used the buttons on his vest to measure their approximate height. As he set up his equipment, he asked questions and listened to the children. Often the workers revealed their names and their real ages and stories about their lives. A seven-year-old boy in Wilmington, Delaware, told Hine that he hauled twenty-five-pound sacks of flour off the delivery wagon. An eight-year-old girl in Alabama explained that she could shuck only two pots of oysters when she had to take care of the baby at the same time. A skilled stenographer, Hine kept notes in a small notebook hidden in his pocket, but only as a way to back up the information revealed in the photographs.

In a single year, Lewis Hine traveled as much as fifty thousand miles. He took pictures of children peddling fruit on city streets; picking cranberries, beets and cotton; shucking oysters; polishing glass in noisy factories; selling newspapers; rolling cigarettes; stringing milk tags; making paper flowers and pillow lace in dingy tenement buildings; working underground in coal mines; and doffing bobbins in textile mills.

By photographing his subjects at their own level, he forced the viewer to look directly into the eyes of the children whose health and education and futures had been sacrificed so that middle-class Americans could live their comfortable lives.

The children in a Hine picture stare out at us with a remarkable mixture of pride, sorrow and pluck. Because Hine sees each one of them as a separate human being, he forces us to do the same. That is why his pictures haunt us to this day.

SEARCHING FOR ADDIE

I first saw the picture of the girl I came to know as Addie at the Bennington Museum in Bennington, Vermont.

She leans on her spinning frame, staring out at the camera, dressed in a filthy smock. Her one pocket is stuffed full. Her left arm rests easily on the frame, but bent at a strange angle, as if perhaps a bone had been broken and was never set properly. Her bare feet, planted firmly, are slick with grease. She looks directly at you, eyes wide open and solemn, her expression resigned, a little wary. She is beautiful.

Addie was just one in an exhibit of child labor photographs taken by Lewis Hine in northern New England. The note he scribbled in his pocket notebook reads "Anemic little spinner in North Pownal Cotton Mill, 1910." Once I saw Addie's face, I never forgot it. My character Grace Forcier was inspired by that face.

Even though I created Grace from my imagination and she grew to be her very own person, I always wondered about Addie. She appears in two group shots Hine took; in both she is pressed right up next to an older girl. The way Addie is leaning on this girl's shoulder makes you think they could be sisters.

But who was Addie? A note by a child labor investigator named E. F. Brown who visited the mill in February 1910 listed her as Addie Laird. In 1998 the U.S. Postal Service issued a stamp showing Addie's picture to commemorate child labor laws in its "Celebrate the Century" series. At that time, researchers at the U.S. Department of Labor admitted they could find no trace of Addie Laird anywhere.

I decided to go looking for her myself. And here's what I found. Starting in 1790 and every decade thereafter, the United States has conducted a census of its citizens. Microfiche copies of these records can be read at the Northeast Office of the National Archives and Record Administration in Pittsfield, Massachusetts. But when I typed "Addie, North Pownal, Vermont, 1910" into the office's computer program, nothing came up. I tried Adeline. No luck. Adelaide. Bingo! The computer screen directed me to one Adalaid Harris, Bennington County, Vermont, roll 1612, page 111, sheet 12B. On the microfiche reader I scrolled through page after page of names penned in a flowery cursive.

There she was. In Pownal, Vermont, Mr. George E. Corey on the fourth day of May, 1910, recorded the two Card sisters: Anna, Female, White, 14 years of age, Single, and Addie, Female, White, 12 years of age, Single. Both were living with their grandmother, a Mrs. Adalaid Harris.

I had found Addie. Her name wasn't Laird; it was Card.

Back in 1910, some shyster sold watered-down ink to the U.S. Department of Labor and Commerce, which was charged with taking the census, so most of the critical information on sheet 12B has simply faded away. But this much I could make out: Anna and Addie were born in Vermont, they spoke English, and they were spinners in the cotton factory. Five other people were also living in the household of Mrs. Adalaid Harris, four of them orphaned or abandoned grandchildren.

Now that I had the correct name, I found Addie again in the 1900 census, living with her widowed father, still in the household of her maternal grandmother. So Addie's mother, Susan Harris, had already died by the time Addie turned two, and by 1910, her father, Emmet D. Card, had disappeared. When I turned to the 1920 census, I could find no Addie Card in the entire country with the correct birth year. This meant one of three things: Addie had either died by the 1920 census, or she had married and her name had been changed, or she had simply slipped through the cracks—as often happens, especially with poorer, rural families.

At this point, I went to the Pownal Town Office, where records of marriages, births, and deaths are kept in a bank vault. The clerks cheerfully dragged out dusty tomes and laid them before me.

I started with the cemetery records, as I was convinced that this frail girl could not have lasted long, considering her twelve-hour days in the mill. I found many Cards in the Pownal graveyards, but no Addie. I scanned burial permits and death records. No Addie.

Just as I was ready to give up, someone offered to look through one more book in the vault. I was halfway out the door when she rushed after me, calling my name. "The book fell open at this page," she said. "I think Addie pushed it off the shelf."

It was Addie Card's marriage certificate.

On February 23, 1915, Addie married Edward Hatch, another spinner in the mill. They were both seventeen.

Now I had her new last name. In the 1920 census, I found her living with the Hatch family and still in the mill, working as a spooler. By that time, her husband, Edward, had joined the navy.

But Addie did not appear in the 1930 census. And because census records are closed for seventy years after they are taken, we won't be able to check the 1940 census until 2010.

At this point, I hired Joe Manning, a friend and fellow writer, to pursue what few leads I had left.

At the end of the trail, we located two of Addie's adoptive descendants. We sat down with them and, in a matter of hours, pieced together the arc of one girl's life. We learned that Addie was sent into the mill when she was eight years old and had to stand on a soapbox to reach the bobbins. She had a nervous collapse at the age of thirteen, just one year after Lewis Hine took her picture. She was tied into her bed while her relatives went to work in the mill. (Could Addie have been "speaking" to me when I imagined Pepe, Grace's grandfather, tied to his bed to keep him from wandering?) We learned that Addie had changed her name to Pat, and that she never knew her own birthday. I handed over a photocopy of the Pownal document that recorded the birth of a baby girl to Susan Harris and Emmet D. Card on December 6, 1898.

Addie never told her descendants about the day Lewis Hine took her picture. She never knew that her face ended up in a Reebok advertisement or on a postage stamp issued a hundred years after her birth or that Hine's original glass-plate negative resides in the Library of Congress. Addie Card never knew that she had become a symbol of the need for child labor reform, and neither did her descendants.

Addie lived the dark side of the American dream. She was married twice, both times unhappily. Months after she lost custody of her biological daughter in 1925, she adopted another girl. They moved often from the mill towns of up-state New York to the big city itself, where Addie and friends were captured in a studio photograph celebrating Victory in Europe Day. By the time Addie died, at ninety-four, she was living in a housing project, surviving on a Social Security check and rent subsidies. But she was rich in the love of her adoptive family. "She didn't have anything to give, but she gave it," her great-granddaughter told us. "I could not imagine my life without Gramma Pat's guidance."

In this novel, history and fiction are pieced together the way Grace twisted the ends of cotton thread to keep her frame running.

We return to the photograph of Addie again and again because Hine saw her not just as a symbol, but also as a person, with a life beyond the mill. For that reason, the "anemic little spinner" remains burned into our national memory as she was etched into the glass of Lewis Hine's negative almost a hundred years ago.

That's why I wrote *Counting on Grace*. And that's why, in the end, I went looking for Addie.

FOR FURTHER READING

Kids at Work: Lewis Hine and the Crusade Against Child Labor, by Russell Freedman, Clarion Books, 1994.

Immigrant Kids, by Russell Freedman, Puffin Books, 1995.

Lewis W. Hine: Children at Work, by Vicki Goldberg, Prestel Publishing, 1999.

America and Lewis Hine: Photographs, 1904–1940, foreword by Walter Rosenblum, Aperture Books/Brooklyn Museum, 1997.

America Through the Lens: Photographers Who Changed the Nation, by Martin W. Sandler, Henry Holt, 2005.

Crusade for the Children: A History of the National Child Labor Committee and Child Labor Reform in America, by Walter I. Trattner, Quadrangle Books, 1970.

Here are some Web sites where you can find information about child labor, as well as other photographs that Lewis Hine took of children in the years 1907 to 1918.

Lewis Hine Collection, Albin O. Kuhn Library, University of Maryland. This site shows Addie's picture, as well as five other photographs that Lewis Hine took in North Pownal in 1910 and notations made on those photographs:

http://aok.lib.umbc.edu/

A brief history of child labor in the United States:
www.historyplace.com/unitedstates/childlabor/

The Library of Congress collections of Hine photographs are cataloged here:
www.loc.gov/rr/print/coll/207-b.html

The National Archives site shows one hundred years of photography from its collections:
www.archives.gov/exhibit_hall/picturing_the_century/portfolios/port_hine.html

The George Eastman House in Rochester, New York, has a large collection of Hine photographs:
www.geh.org/fm/1whprints/htmlsrc2/

ACKNOWLEDGMENTS

While they cannot be held responsible for any errors I have made in the telling of this story, I wish to thank the following individuals, who were generous with their time and expertise:

John Goodwin, who took a great deal of time to help me understand the workings of the spinning frame and the process of textile production in general. His patience and his technical knowledge proved invaluable.

Linda Hall, a researcher and librarian herself, who steered me in many helpful directions, from unpublished information on French Canadians in New England to details about the town of North Pownal to help with finding Addie.

Ken and Joyce Held of the North Pownal Historical Society, who have been enthusiastic supporters of this project from the beginning and who work tirelessly to give their community a sense of its unique history.

Nichole Frocheur, for her detailed description of the developing process for glass-plate negatives and her close reading of the manuscript.

Betty Boudreau, who took time from her busy life to give me a tour of North Pownal.

Rob Niederman, a camera historian, who gave generously

of his time and expertise in helping me to understand the workings of cameras and the developing process in Hine's era.

Todd Gustavson of the George Eastman House, for answers to specific questions about Lewis Hine's equipment and techniques.

Debbie Sprague, who showed me her own personal research on her French Canadian heritage.

DISCLAIMERS

Experts disagree on exactly which camera Lewis Hine used in 1910. He did own a five-by-seven-inch Graflex later in his career, and I could not resist the temptation of having Grace meet "Mr. Graflex," since their names shared those first three letters.

In actual fact, in 1910, the State of Vermont did not require proof of age when children came into the mills, but the practice of demanding birth certificates varied from one factory to the next, depending on who was the superintendent and how recently a state labor investigator had visited.

Although I have set my story in North Pownal, Vermont, in a cotton textile mill that functioned there from the 1860s through the 1930s, I have changed certain geographical and historical details of the town and surrounding area.

As I always say when writing historical fiction, I'm not saying it happened, I'm saying it could have happened.

ABOUT THE AUTHOR

Elizabeth Winthrop is the bestselling author of more than fifty books for readers of all ages, including the award-winning classic *The Castle in the Attic* and its sequel, *The Battle for the Castle*. Her popular picture books include *Dumpy La Rue*, *Dog Show*, and *Shoes*. Her most recent novel for middle-grade readers, *The Red-Hot Rattoons*, is a comic fantasy set in New York City, where the author makes her home for half the year. For the remaining months, she lives in northwestern Massachusetts, two miles from the small Vermont mill town where *Counting on Grace* is set.